Playing the Game

The Making the Play Series

L.M. Reid

Happy Reading!
L. M. Reid

SCARLET LANTERN
Publishing

Scarlet Lantern Publishing

Prologue

Quinn

When I step into the lecture hall, Professor Powell's eyes fall on me. I would be lying if I said that the slight smirk on his lips and subtle shake of his head wasn't a turn on. Not when I know that it's because he's remembering exactly what happened at our so-called "study session" last night.

A study session, where he was supposed to do exactly that, help me study.

Not that I needed it. No, that was all just a ruse.

When I showed up to his office last night, I had anything but studying on my mind. In fact...

I open my trench coat, the lace panties and bra underneath the only clothing I have on.

"Quinn, what are you doing?" Professor Powell asks. I've clearly surprised him. The way his eyes rake over me though, I'm fairly certain he won't be complaining.

I saunter over to him. I scrape my nails along his chest, straight down to his waistband. "What does it look like I'm doing... Professor?"

A smile plays on his lips. His hands grip my hips and hoist me onto his desk. He steps between my legs.

"You've not been behaving in class, Ms. Ford. I'm going to have to give you a bad grade for that."

I spread my legs further as I worry my lip between my teeth. "Isn't there anything else I could do, professor? I hate being in trouble."

He flicks the clasp on my bra open, freeing my breasts. "I might be able to think of something."

"Quit fantasizing, Ms. Ford, and take your seat," the Professor tells me.

I glance around the room that's now filled up. While his words have a meaning to me, they seem innocent enough to the rest of the class. Unless of course they knew I was staring at him.

Honestly, though. I don't even care.

Teacher-student relationships are frowned upon. But I'll be damned if Professor Powell isn't worth it.

At his request, I take my seat. My phone flashes a message from him.

Professor: Good girl following directions. After class I'll give you a reward.

My thighs clench at the thought. Christ, I want him.

After class, Quinn. All you have to do is make it through class. Not a hard feat considering I get to stare at the Professor the entire time.

He begins his lecture and I allow myself to drift back to last night. Every position, every taste, every last....

"Where is she?" a woman's voice shouts.

The door to the lecture hall slams behind her with a thud.

"Amber?" Professor Powell, otherwise known as Shane, asks.

I turn to look where everyone else's eyes have already drifted to – to the beautiful woman standing in the entrance to the lecture hall. Her blonde hair is pulled back and her clothes are pressed and professional. Even from a distance I can see that her eyes are filled with fury and her cheeks are flushed a deep red. She's pissed. And since her eyes are glued to Shane, I can only assume it's him that she's pissed at.

"Where is she?" the woman shouts again.

The entire class has their eyes on her, but mine are on Shane. The panicked look in his eyes, the fear etched onto his face.

"Where is she?" the woman demands again.

"This isn't the time or place," he tells her. Not that she cares in the slightest. She is filled with such a rage that there isn't anything that will calm her except finding the woman she's looking for.

That's when I realize that the woman she's looking for, is me. And that Shane is married. He's fucking married. And I feel like such a bitch.

I might be the kind of girl who's going to screw her professor, but I am not the girl who has affairs with married men. Or even just taken men. I've been on the losing end of the cheating realm more times than I can count, and I would never do that to anyone. Not that it will matter to her. It sure as hell never mattered to me.

Amber's eyes begin to dart around the room and when they fall on me, I freeze.

Shit.

"You," she yells. "You little bitch."

In the blink of an eye the woman, Amber, is standing in front of me. She's yelling and screaming and creating a scene. And I let her because I deserve it.

"I had no idea he was married," I tell her. Not that it will do any good. The anger and sadness that she is feeling isn't going to dissipate just because I didn't know.

Shane reaches us and his hands reach for her. His words are soft and smooth in an attempt to calm her. "Amber, honey, listen..."

I cringe at his words, the way he's trying to placate her. I've been in her shoes before. And the way he's talking to her, that's not going to bode well for him.

"I am so sorry," I tell her. And it's not just some bullshit line to try and calm her or get her to not punch me. If I were her, I would have done it already.

The truth is, I am sorry. I am sorry that she's hurting, I'm sorry that he cheated, and most of all I'm sorry because I had no fucking clue. If I had, I wouldn't have gotten involved with him. There are plenty of sexy single professors.

"I bet you are," she says. The sting of her hand against my cheek stops me from speaking.

Nothing I say or do is going to make it better, so I let her have her moment. I let her take her anger out on me now, hoping like hell that she lets him have it later.

I really like Shane. Despite the teacher-student thing, I really thought maybe one day we could have something.

Turns out all we have is a real fucking mess.

Chapter 1

Quinn

"What do you mean you got kicked out of school?" Mason shouts at me.

He may only be a few years older than me, but he took on the parental role when our parents didn't bother to. Our childhood was a shitshow, only made better by the fact that Mason was an amazing older brother who did everything in his power to make sure we were taken care of.

I sit on his couch, staring at my hands, unsure how to tell him the "how" that I know he is going to be asking about next.

He's pacing in front of me. He always paces when he's trying to figure shit out. Right now, he's probably wondering how I could have turned all his hard work and sacrifices into this mess. All I had to do was follow my dream. He would take care of the rest.

And I threw it all away for sex.

That is an admission I am not quite ready to make.

"Why? How? What in the fuck did you do, Quinn?"

Mason might be used to my wild ways – shitty boyfriends, partying too hard. But this? Getting kicked out of a school that I worked my ass off to get into? Even this is a bit much for me.

After the whole fiasco in the classroom with Professor Powell and his wife, rumors started to fly. My grades were brought into question. After all, how does the whorish girl who slept with her professor also manage to have straight A's? Why, she must have screwed her way to them.

"If I were you, I would strongly consider changing schools."

That was the Dean's recommendation. After all the looks and comments, I couldn't help but to agree.

"I wasn't kicked out so much as it was suggested that I switch schools," I tell him.

It took every ounce of courage I have to even call Mason and tell him that I needed a place to stay because I had to leave school and, in turn, my dorm room. Even through the phone I could feel the anger radiating off him. Everything he sacrificed, everything he did so I could make my dreams come true. So that we could both have a better life. And what do I do? I go and throw it all away.

The blink of an eye.

That's all it took.

Mason demanded that I come back here to Remington. Not that I had much of a choice as there was no place else for me to go. The only other directive – I need to get my shit together.

That's a given.

A given or not, it's not going to be easy. I'm the screw up. He's the good guy. It's always been like that. Where he had to take charge and be responsible, I acted out. I could because I knew he would always take care of it. And he has. Except this time, I may have pushed the envelope a little too far. Getting kicked out of school is a far cry from my usual behavior - shitfaced at a party or dating assholes.

"I know you're disappointed in me," I tell him.

Finally, he takes a seat next to me. "I'm not disappointed. Hell, I'm not even mad."

I raise my eyebrows at him knowing that last line is bullshit. He's pissed. It's written all over his face.

"Okay, maybe I'm a little mad. But, mostly, I'm just worried about you, Q."

We always swore that we were going to make a better life for ourselves. While Mason has managed to accomplish that, I'm still trying to find my way. Usually through sex and booze and partying.

"I don't know what's going on with you, Q, and honestly, I don't care what happened at Columbia. I just want to move forward. I want to help you make something of yourself because you are way too talented to throw your life away because of some bullshit."

I smile at him, loving the fatherly speech he just gave me and hating it all at the same time.

"I will get my shit together, I promise."

How I'm going to do that exactly, I have no idea. Though, based on the look on his face, I'm fairly certain he's about to tell me.

"Good. For starters, you're going to enroll at Remington University. I don't care what you go to school for, but you're going to school."

I nod in agreement. I don't have a choice. No money, no job, no choice but to rely on my brother to take care of me. Again.

You would think that would be incentive enough to keep me on the straight and narrow, yet here I am having made a mess of things.

"You're not her," he says. To most, it would seem like his comment comes out of left field. But to me? It makes total sense. "Just like I'm not him. We can do better. We can make a life for ourselves."

Mason, the protector. The eternal optimist.

If he only knew how much more I am like our mother then he realizes, he would hate me. It's a truth that just might destroy us.

I pull back from the embrace and smile at my brother. The man who is already doing it – proving himself. Not only did he make it into the NFL, he's crushing it. Looking at Mason now though, I'm determined to turn it around. To do good if for no other reason than to allow him the ability to not have to worry about me so he can live out his dream. In the least, I can make a good show of it.

That much I'm certain of.

"I know," I say only to pacify him.

He pulls me in for a hug. As he squeezes every last breath out of me, he says. "I'm not glad you got kicked out of school, but I'm glad you're here. I missed you."

I hug him back. "I missed you, too."

When he pulls back, he smiles at me, the anger gone. "Come on, let me show you to your room."

He grabs my bags and leads me down the long hallway to a spacious bedroom. Mason drops my bag on the bed. "So, what do you think?"

The room looks way too nice, way too decorated for him to have done it himself. "I love it." I turn to face him. "How is Avery by the way?"

I can tell by the touches around the room that she played a part in this. I also know my brother well enough to know that outside of me and his friend Hunter, Avery is the only other person he would let close enough to even have a say in it.

The sound of her name brings an instantaneous smile to his face. One that I'm certain he doesn't even realize happens.

"She's good. Doing really well, actually. She's going to be thrilled to have you around."

"I can't wait to see her either," I say with a smile.

"You know you can talk to me, right? You can tell me anything? I just want to help," Mason says.

I wrap my arms around my brother and hug him again. "I'm well aware. I promise you, Mase, I'm okay. I fucked up, but I'm okay. And I won't let it happen again. I will make you proud of me one of these days."

Mason shakes his head. "I'm already proud of you, Quinn. I just wish you would take a minute to be proud of yourself."

Mason leaves the room, his words left behind to rattle around in my head.

Chapter 2

Hunter

Sliding the key into the lock, I let myself into Mason's condo. He and Avery should be here soon. When they are, we will be heading out to pick up Layla for the charity event.

As I make my way into the living room, I can't help but notice that the usually messy space is immaculate. Avery must have cleaned up after his ass again. I don't know why in the hell she does it. Then I smile to myself thinking about all the shit I put up with from Mason. There's just something about the guy. His never-ending faith. His loyalty. Even after the shit life he and his sister grew up in, he persevered. So, if he needs a little extra looking after on occasion, so be it. I owe him enough to put up with it.

Just as I'm about to turn the corner, something, or rather someone, runs directly into me. My hands grip soft skin as my eyes drift down.

Quinn Ford.

Trouble with a capital T.

She lets out a scream before realizing who it is that she ran into. The moment she does, her hand connects with my arm, swatting me away. Seeing her standing in front of me wearing nothing but a towel has me completely dumbfounded. I'm stunned, and in a hell of a lot of trouble considering I've been staring at her longer than I should.

"What are you doing here?" she asks. She places her hands on her hips, causing the towel to slide down ever so slightly. I fake a cough to hide the groan that escapes.

"Me? What about you? Shouldn't you be off at school?"

Quinn attends Columbia University. She's an art major, and a talented one from what I've heard. So why in the hell is she here when she should be there?

Rather than answer my question, she deflects. "Haven't you ever heard of knocking?"

I clear my throat as I hold up the key. "I have, but usually don't since I have one of these."

It's the key that Mason gave me to his place, just like the one I gave him to mine. It's also a key I have zero intention of using again until long after Quinn leaves.

She steps forward, grabbing the key out of my hand. "Now you don't, so you can leave."

"Oh no you don't," I say as I grab her wrist.

We struggle slightly for the key, a struggle that undoubtedly, I will win. I'm bigger. I'm stronger. Yet, I am so much weaker because the moment I see her towel beginning to slip, I let the key go and turn around.

"Shit," I curse as I divert my eyes from her naked body. I do it for a lot of reasons, but the most important being I have a girlfriend. I have for a long time. One that I love. And everything about seeing Quinn in her state of undress feels wrong. So damn wrong. Especially since a part of me wants to keep on looking even though I know I shouldn't.

I can't.

I won't.

"What? You've never seen a naked woman before?" Quinn asks with a laugh.

"Go put some damn clothes on," I instruct her, my eyes staring at the front door praying that Mason doesn't walk in. All I need is for him to get the wrong impression, or worse, for Layla to walk in with him. I can only imagine how she would react if she saw Quinn and me together like this.

Quinn has always been defiant, so when she actually does as I ask, I'm notably surprised. When I hear the door to her bedroom shut, I turn around and scrub my hand over my face.

Holy hell, what was that? And why did I like it so much?

I plop down on the couch and grab the remote. I need a distraction. Any distraction. Even something as trivial as the stupid reality show that's playing.

"Better?" Quinn asks when she returns to the living room. Her arms are outstretched as she does a little twirl.

"Much," I lie. Because despite the clothing she's wearing, I'm still picturing the slight glimpse I got of her naked body. Every glorious inch of it. "I didn't realize you were visiting Mason."

"I'm not," she says.

"Then what are you doing here?"

She looks down at her hands as she speaks. The always confident and wild girl is seemingly uncharacteristically meek. "I... uh... I'm staying here for a while."

"Why? Did you get kicked out of school or something?" I tease. Or at least I think I'm teasing until she doesn't respond, her gaze still focused on her hands. "Holy shit, what did you do?"

"None of your business," she says. Her voice is argumentative and snippy as she responds. She makes a face at me before heading into the kitchen.

I follow her in there. "Oh, come on, just tell me. You know I'm going to find out anyway."

"I failed, okay? Are you happy?"

"Why would that make me happy?" I ask, confused by her question. I know we don't exactly get along, but does she honestly believe that I want her to fail?

"Because it proves what you already know."

"And what exactly is that? Because aside from knowing you're a pain in my ass, I don't know a damn thing about you, Quinn. Just like you don't know a thing about me."

She takes a sip out of the bottled water she grabbed from the fridge. "I know plenty about you, Hunter."

There is such disdain in her voice. I have no clue where it comes from or how it started. "Such as?" I ask as I fold my arms across my chest.

"Enough."

I roll my eyes at her lack of response. It's all she can give me because I'm starting to think that even she doesn't know why she hates me so much.

The phone sitting on the counter next to me begins to ring. Quinn dashes for it, but I pull it out of her reach.

"Who's Shane?" I ask as I glance down at the caller ID.

"None of your business. Give me back my phone," Quinn orders me. Not that I plan on following her direction. Not until she answers my question. Honestly.

"Not until you tell me the real reason that you left Columbia because we both know it had nothing to do with your grades."

The phone stops ringing. The call...missed. And Quinn? Well, rather than fighting for the phone, she walks away and returns to her bottle of water.

"Come on, fess up already," I say as I follow her.

"Even if you're right, not that I'm saying you are... what in the hell makes you think I would tell you?"

I shrug my shoulders. I have no idea why she would tell me. Just like I have no idea why she hates me.

"I'm just trying to help," I say as I slide her phone across the island to her.

"Oh, please. Like you give a damn about what happens to me."

"If I didn't, Quinn, I wouldn't be asking."

Admitting I give a damn about her is enough to silence her. At least for a moment. Then she's right back to her snarky comments. "I don't need you or your concern."

"Why do you hate me? Why do you always think every attempt I make at being your friend has some sort of malicious intent behind it? Because I assure you, Quinn, that is not the case."

"You being you is more than enough reason for me to not like you. Sorry if that's hard for you to swallow, but it's the truth," she says as she tries to move past me.

I step in front of her, my unwillingness to let this go overshadowing my need to not fight with her. "How can you say that? You don't know me. You never gave me a chance."

"A chance to what? Prove me right?"

I look her dead in the eyes. "To prove to you that not everyone is like your parents. Not every man is like the assholes you date. There are good people out there, Quinn. You just have to give them a chance."

My words strike a nerve in her, putting her even more on the defensive and standing here, toe to toe. We're already on the verge of world war three.

"What don't you get, hmm? My life is my business. Not yours. Stay out of it."

"I'm just trying to be nice. To be your friend."

"I don't need you to be my friend, or my protector, or anything else for that matter."

"Fine," I say, throwing my hands up in the air. "I'm tired of trying with you. I can't win."

"Finally, he gets it."

"Loud and clear."

The question is, why in the hell do I care? Why is the fact that she won't let me in bothering me so much?

"You stay out of my life and I will stay out of yours."

While that is exactly what I should do, what I always should have done, the sadness that I see in her eyes, the deep seeded pain I know she feels – I can't. I can't walk away from her. Just like I couldn't walk away from Mason. Not then. Not now.

"What the hell is going on now?" Mason's voice asks from the doorway. Avery is standing next to him.

"Nothing," I reply.

"Just Hunter being Hunter."

I shake my head at her immature response. Her bullshit excuse for why she hates me. Me being me is enough? What does that even mean? "Can we go?"

Mason shakes his head and turns his attention to Quinn. "You want to come with us? It's a great event, I really think you'd enjoy it."

"I am not going anywhere with him," she replies as she walks past me toward her room.

I stalk off in the other direction but stop to glance behind me just before I walk out of Mason's.

"You want to tell me what we walked in on?" Mason asks.

"Nope. Not worth the time. Besides, we need to go, Layla's waiting."

Quinn Ford is not my problem. Never was. Never will be.

Chapter 3

Hunter

She's not my problem.

At least that's what I keep telling myself regardless of the fact that since our argument last week, I haven't been able to get her and whatever it is that she's hiding off my mind.

"So, what do you think it is?" I ask Mason, inquiring about the very thing that I keep telling myself I don't care about.

Seems I'm not the only one questioning what brought Quinn to Mason's doorstep. He's not buying her story either.

"I don't know, man. But the last report she sent me was amazing. She was acing everything."

I push my legs out on the leg press, then slowly retract them. I grunt with the strength it takes for them to not buckle. "Maybe she's lying? Maybe she wasn't kicked out. Maybe she quit."

Maybe it was because of some asshole guy who treated her badly? And just how badly did he treat her? I push harder one last time letting at whoever hurt Quinn fuel my drive.

Mason shrugs. "Even if that was the case. Why? She was doing so well. I don't know. I don't get it."

"Quinn ever mention someone named Shane?" I ask, recalling our last conversation.

"No, why?"

I shake my head. "Never mind."

"You think it's because of some guy?"

I shrug. "No. Maybe. I'm don't know. I've never understood your sister."

"You and me both," Mason says with a laugh. "I just wish she would tell me what's going on so I could help."

"Maybe she doesn't want your help," I say as I pat him on the back.

Quinn has always gone by the beat of her own drum. She's fiercely independent and hates being told what to do. It doesn't take a genius to see that her having to stay with Mason, to rely on him, is killing her. Despite her attitude, that says otherwise.

"Just think, there's only a couple more weeks to the wedding. Then you can forget about Quinn and relax. Focus on fun, sun, and..."

"Women, all the women," Mason replies as he claps his hands together.

"What happened to you bringing Avery?" I ask. Avery McCall is Mason's other best friend. She's also the only woman other than Quinn that has managed to hold his attention for more than a few hours.

"I was," he says. He pauses, which is a clear indication that I'm not going to like whatever it is he says next. "But the more I thought about the more I realized it wasn't fair to her."

"Really? Why is that?"

"I'm going to be busy feasting on the bridesmaid buffet and Avery won't have anyone to hang out with."

"Bridesmaid buffet? Jesus Christ, Mase." I shake my head as I laugh. "You're a damn mess."

"It's not like that's a newsflash."

The fact that Mason has commitment issues isn't shocking. Not with the parents he grew up with. A father who, when he was around, was drunk or high and a mother who usually brought a different man home every night to help support her husband's habit. It's amazing that the two of them turned out as well as they did.

"Besides, at least someone will be here to keep an eye on Quinn," Mason says.

Keeping an eye on Quinn wasn't an issue for me. Tearing my eyes away from her towel clad body was. I still feel guilty for that. Looking at another woman when the woman of my dreams was at home getting ready for me.

Unable to talk to Mason about my little transgression for obvious reasons, I turned to my brother, Hudson. He assured me that looking, and touching, are two different things and that what I did wasn't awful. Still, I felt wrong and I felt like shit. Enough that I decided to plan a special night for me and Layla tonight.

"What were you and Quinn fighting about the other night anyway?" Mason asks, breaking through my thoughts.

"What don't we fight about?" I laugh. "I just don't get why she hates me."

"I don't think she hates you. I think she resents you for having what we didn't. She tries to act tough, but all that shit affects her more than she lets on."

Me being me.

His explanation makes sense. But there has to be more. Something I'm not seeing.

As soon as I think it, I feel guilty again. Why in the hell am I worrying about Quinn when I have Layla waiting for me at home?

"Yeah, well, if you ask her, she hates me. And I'm done trying to make her feel otherwise," I tell him.

Everyone has already made it back to the locker room while Mason and I finish up the extra workout we always do. It's the same routine we've done our whole lives. Whatever anyone else does, we do more. We work to succeed. I'll be damned if the guy doesn't push me to do it every time. Sometimes I swear he's the only reason that I made it to the NFL. Not so much because of the work we put in, but just his drive and determination. If he set the goal for us, there was no way we weren't going to accomplish it.

"I don't blame you for that one," he says. "I just wish I could figure her out."

"If you haven't by now, I'm pretty sure you should just give up to. Go with the flow and be by her side, man. That's all you can do."

"If only she would meet a nice guy, someone who would help her give up this wild partying streak of hers."

I give him a side eye. "Pot, meet kettle."

"I already have my shit together," he says in defense of his antics. The ones that don't differ much from hers. The very reason he's been deemed the bad boy, player of the Red Devils.

Those same antics are also the very reason why he gives me shit all the time about Layla.

Speaking of...

I glance at the clock on the wall then back at Mason. "Last set. I need to get home."

"Awe, is Layla waiting for you?" he says in this sing songy voice.

"As a matter of fact, yes."

"Pussy whipped," he coughs out.

"It's called being in love. You should try it. It's pretty damn amazing," I say even though I know it makes me sound just like that – a pussy whipped lover boy. The mere thought of Layla has me not disputing him. For her, I'll be that guy.

Chapter 4

Hunter

A s I step through the door to my apartment, the first thing I hear is her laughter. It's like music to my ears. I step inside and revel at just how much I love her laugh, her voice, everything about her. Layla Malone is everything I ever wanted in a woman – and more.

Before I even reach the door to the bedroom, I can picture her in there, cuddled under the covers the remote in her hand, and whatever stupid sitcom it is that she's watching on the television.

I push the bedroom door open, "Hey, baby."

The visual I just had is far from the one that's laid out before me. Layla's in bed alright, but she sure as hell isn't watching television. As I stare absently at the scene before me trying to process what in the hell is happening, my duffle bag drops from my hand in a thud that snaps me back to reality. My mouth falls open and I swear every last breath of air leaves my body. My world is spinning, my heart is racing, and the woman I love is currently having sex with some other guy. In my bed. And all I can think to do is ask her what's going on when that is already abundantly clear.

She gasps, then says my name as a surprised exclamation. Why she seems so surprised, I'm not sure because it's my damn apartment she's fucking him in. She doesn't even live here.

As I stand there trying to process everything, I realize that she hasn't even moved. He's still inside her. That's fine by me because I sure as hell never will be again. Fuck this. Fuck her.

Unable to stand by and witness any more than I already have I say, "Leave your key when you're finished."

I can hear her call after me just before the door to the apartment slams shut behind me.

I stalk down the hallway taking the stairs in hopes of burning off some of the anger raging inside me. I make my way through the lobby of my building and straight into something. Or rather, someone.

"Jesus, Hunter, where's the fire?" I hear Quinn bark out at me.

I blink my eyes a few times still trying to gauge what the hell is going on.

"Hey, are you okay?" she asks. There is concern in her eyes and seeing it there almost makes me laugh. The idea of Quinn being concerned for me is beyond absurd. I stare at her for a second more before continuing on my path until I'm outside. Stepping into the fresh air, I finally stop and take a breath.

"Can I bring you your car, Mr. Adams?" the valet asks.

I glance around me. Cars flying by, people walking down the street hand in hand. The sounds of the city filling my head.

"I'll walk."

I pull the ball cap on my head down further and make my way down the street. I walk aimlessly for what feels like hours. The entire time my mind trying to grasp what went wrong, how in the hell Layla and I got here. Even the city sounds can't drown out the incessant sound of the messages coming through on my phone. I glance down at it, texts from Layla and Mason lighting up the screen.

And now Quinn decides to be a decent human being? To try and help me when I don't want help when all I want is to drown in my sorrows?

Alcohol. That's what I need.

Needing to be somewhere alone I bypass the bars where undoubtedly, I will know people. I'm the defensive end for the Remington Red Devils. Everyone knows me and the last thing I need tonight is to go to a place where everybody knows my name.

I spot the Regency Hotel out of the corner of my eye. It's perfect. No one ever frequents the hotel bars. Not to mention, I'm going to need a place to sleep tonight. There is no way in hell I can go back to that apartment. Not yet. Not when the visual is so strong, the sheets too messy.

The bartender eyes me as I take a seat at the bar. It's obvious he recognizes me, but he doesn't question it or make a scene. Thank fuck for that.

"Whiskey, on the rocks," I say flatly.

I'm not much of a drinker to begin with. Maybe a beer here or there. But I definitely don't dive into the hard stuff. But tonight? Tonight, sure as hell warrants something stronger than a beer. Something that will hopefully dull the ache in my chest and the visual in my head. I down the drink the minute he sets it in front of me.

"Another."

Another drink down. Another drink ordered. And even less clue as to what the fuck just happened? How did I end up here? What went wrong between Layla and I that she would do this? We were happy, or at least, I thought we were. I was. Why wasn't she? Had I missed something?

I scrub my hand over my face and rack my brain trying to figure it out. But the more I think, the angrier I become because the only real way for me to know is to ask her. No way. Not happening. If I never lay eyes on her again, it will be too soon.

The phone I had been ignoring all evening flashes with more missed messages. All from the same number. I don't read the texts, but I respond anyway.

Me: *Make sure you change the sheets before you go. Oh, and burn the old ones while you're at it.*

Then I turn the damn thing off and return to drowning in my sorrows.

When I demand another drink, the bartender raises an eyebrow at me. "Please?" I grit out the words trying to make them sound as nice as possible.

He shakes his head and laughs but brings me a double this time. "It's not going to make it go away," he tells me. "She might, though."

I look in the direction that he nods his head, the sexy woman with black hair, electric blue streaks, and a dress that leaves little to my imagination.

Fucking hell could this night get any worse?

That woman that the bartender just nodded to, isn't any woman. In fact, she's not even old enough to be in this damn bar, though I'm fairly certain her ID says otherwise.

Quinn.

"Not happening," I tell the bartender and chuckle slightly at the thought of it.

Don't get me wrong, Quinn is stunning. Deep emerald eyes, long legs, and a smile that is simultaneously sweet and full of mischief. And since seeing her in that towel, I have admittedly thought about it more than I should have.

The thing about Quinn is – she makes you do stupid things. And I don't do stupid things. I pride myself on being a good guy, a stand-up guy. Quinn is trouble and not the kind that I need to be getting into.

Yet, I can't seem to take my eyes off her. She's sitting alone at a table, her eyes focused on the phone before her. It looks like she's waiting for someone. But who? What the hell is going on with her?

As I continue to stare, some guy covered in tattoos approaches her. She smiles politely, but even from where I'm sitting it's obvious that she isn't interested. Tattoo guy doesn't seem to care though. He just keeps pressing and pushing. I let it go until I see his hand on her arm. She tries to tug it away, but it doesn't work.

I stand, the alcohol hitting me a little harder than I thought it would. I shake of the unsteady feeling and head in their direction just in time to hear Quinn tell the man she isn't interested.

"I believe the lady said no," I say.

The guy looks up and laughs. "Fuck off."

"Can't do that. Not until you let her go," I tell him.

He shoves Quinn to the side. "And who the fuck do you think you are?"

I'm a guy looking for a fight. And Quinn – yep, she's definitely the kind of woman that makes you do stupid things. Like cock your arm back and punch the tattooed asshole in the face. When he falls to the ground, Quinn rushes to my side.

"Jesus, Hunter, are you okay?" she asks.

I shake off the sting from my hand. "I'm fine."

The bartender comes up next to us, security following closely behind.

He lets out a small laugh as he rests his hand on my shoulder, "Like I said."

I look down at Quinn, her mouth having fallen lax and her eyes wide as she stares up at me. "What?"

"I didn't think you had it in you," she says, a smile appearing on her face.

I shake my head. "I don't know why I bother."

I head back over to the bar and take my seat. And a drink.

"Thank you," a soft voice next to me says. While I know it's hers, I can't help but be confused by it. The gentle sound is unfamiliar to me when usually her voice is filled with anger or contempt or anything but kindness when it's directed at me. There is a vulnerability there that pulls me in when it shouldn't.

"Have a seat," I say. "Drinks are on me."

"You want me to join you?"

I shrug.

Do I? I mean, Quinn and I, we've never spent a minute alone together. Hell, that one sentence without a dig or her yelling is probably the longest bout of civility we've ever had. But this being alone thing isn't helping. Maybe bartender guy over here is right, maybe listening to her ramble, or yell, or give me shit will help. Whatever she says can't be worse than the ache I feel in my chest.

"What are you doing here?" Quinn asks as she slides into the seat next to me.

I let out a groan when her leg brushes against mine. The sensation the feeling of her against me gives is almost too good.

"What's going on? Why are you sitting in a hotel bar, completely wasted?" she pries again.

"I'm not that drunk." The slur of my words and the several empty glasses in front of me say otherwise. I'm not sure if it's the alcohol, or just having someone familiar here to vent to but despite not wanting to talk to Quinn I blurt out that Layla and I broke up.

She doesn't seem fazed by my admission. There is no pity or sadness in her eyes. I shouldn't be surprised, the two of them don't exactly get along. And God knows I am not Quinn's favorite person. All the more reason that I question her motives, and her continued interest in my dilemma. "Okay... but why are you hiding out here?"

"Because we broke up while she was fucking some guy in my apartment, so I don't quite feel like being there. Happy?"

"Hunter, I'm so sorry." Her hand rests on my arm and it takes everything in me not to yank it away. For whatever reason, her touch, the nearness of her, it's having a strange effect on me. Maybe it's the alcohol or my jumbled-up feelings about Layla, but Christ her touch feels way too damn good right now.

"Thanks. What about you? What are you doing here?"

"I was supposed to meet someone, but it looks like they're not going to show."

"Shane?" I ask recalling the name from her phone the other night. She nods.

"Does he have something to do with why you left Columbia?" I ask curiosity getting the best of me.

"We were doing so well, too," she says as she shifts in her chair and looks away from me. Her tone, her body language, it all changes at my intrusion into her personal life.

"I'm sorry, I didn't mean to pry. I'm just trying to make conversation." That, and, I'm curious. So damn curious and I don't have a clue why.

She rolls her eyes, nothing that I didn't expect. "It's complicated."

"Isn't it always," I chuckle. Visions of Layla and the guy she was with still too clear in my mind. The alcohol isn't helping. Not yet at least.

My hand grips my refilled glass and I hold it up in a toast. "Fuck relationships."

"Fuck relationships," she repeats as she clinks her glass against mine. We drink. Then she blows my mind. "For what it's worth, I think you can do better."

Laughter bubbles over. "Oh, really?"

She grabs the drink the bartender just set in front of her and brings it to her lips. My eyes focus on her lips as she takes a sip of the amber liquid. Gorgeous red lips that look so damn good I want to taste them. Christ, the bartender was right. She could make me forget all my damn problems.

"Layla is way too stuck up for you. You need someone who will..."

"Will what?" I ask. As I lean in closer, her scent wafts over me. Fuck she smells delicious. Good enough to eat. The thought instantly has me wanting to bury my head between her thighs and do just that.

Whoa where did that come from? I really must be more drunk than I realize if I'm that's even a thought in my head.

"Teach you how to have a little fun."

I grab a strand of her hair and play with it. "Believe me Quinn, I know how to have... fun."

Quinn's eyes widen at the words and the suggestion behind them. Holy shit, did I just flirt with her?

She looks at me with an amused smile on her face. Before she can speak though, before she fucks up this moment with a snarky comment, I kiss her. I press my lips softly against hers because drunk or not, I'm not the guy that takes what isn't returned. Her hand grips my arm a little harder, those lips I wanted to taste returning the favor.

Christ do they ever know how to kiss.

The hurt and anger I feel toward Layla mixed with the new and insatiable desire I seem to be experiencing for Quinn has me in a damn tailspin.

I pull back and look into her eyes. The permission I need is granted in the way she's looking at me. Any other night, I would walk away. I would respect my friendship with Mason, honor my feelings for Layla. But not tonight.

Tonight, I just want to feel something good. Quinn sure as fuck feels good.

I slam some money on the counter and grab her hand. "Let's get out of here."

"What? Where are we going?" She might be questioning what the hell is happening, but she is still following.

Chapter 5

Quinn

I'm pretty sure I know where Hunter's going and where this whole evening is leading. The thing I don't understand is why in the world I am following so willingly.

Maybe it has something to do with the fact that Shane didn't show. That despite my nonchalance about everything, I liked him. And finding out he was married hurt me. Then tonight, he convinced me to meet him and against my better judgment I agreed. Like a damn fool, I allowed him to hurt me yet again.

Hunter rests his hand on the small of my back as we stand before the elevator, the insignificant touch searing me. His intentions are clear. To finish what he started with that kiss. And God do I want him to. I want this man that I have spent most of my life hating more than I want my next breath.

I press my back to his front, the hardness of his cock presses against me and causes me to moan. "Impressive."

"You haven't seen anything yet," he whispers into my ear. The sound sends a shiver down my body.

The elevator chimes. I enter and turn to face Hunter. He's standing there, hands holding the doors open, eyes filled with uncertainty as he stares at me. Then something changes. As though a flip switches in him, Hunter takes two strides and joins me in the elevator his body pressing against mine, backing me up against the wall.

"Fuck it," he murmurs just before his lips crash against mine.

I part my lips allowing him further access to explore, taste, and take whatever it is he wants from me. For the first time in my life I truly feel alive. Everything about Hunter Adams consumes me.

The elevator dings and the doors open when we arrive at his floor. This is my last chance to walk away and end whatever the hell this is that we're doing. Something that is obviously so wrong but feels so right.

Hunter doesn't press. In fact, he doesn't even speak. He just stands there, looking at me with these amazing blue eyes, waiting for me to make the decision. Somehow it doesn't really feel like a decision I can make, but rather one that's already been made for me. Because without so much as an ounce of hesitation, I step off the elevator with him, walk to his room and step inside.

"What are we doing?" I ask when I turn to face him.

I hate Hunter and I'm pretty sure the feeling is mutual. Right now, though, he's somehow healing everything inside of me.

He looks as confused as I do. "Hell, if I know."

That uncertainty doesn't stop him though. In an instant he is on me again, lips moving with mine, hands exploring every inch of me. Christ the man is amazing. My legs wrap around him, his hardness pressing into my core. He grinds against me and I lose whatever restraint I have left.

"Now, Hunter. I need you now." Desperation fills my voice and the sound of it must be the last bit of fuel that was needed to ignite this fire.

He carries me to the bed, dropping me onto the plush padding. Standing over me, he tears his shirt over his head and discards it onto the floor.

There is something primal in the way he's looking at me. Something so dangerous and sexy and when he's fully unclothed, he maneuvers his body over my still clothed one. With the skirt of my dress shoved up around my waist, he runs a finger over my entrance. He growls out my name before claiming my lips again.

I can feel the latex wrapped head of his cock at my already soaked entrance. I cry out when he pushes into me. The length, the girth, every inch of him stretching me beyond comprehension. My eyes go hazy as the sting of pain turns to pleasure.

We move in sync, a natural, almost instinctual knowledge of what the other wants and how they want it taking over.

There's no more ache in my heart, sheer pleasure consumes me. Hunter consumes me. When breaks the kiss and looks into my eyes, I become undone. There in that look is something I've never seen before, never experienced in my life. Adoration. As though, whatever this is, means something to him. Like I am more than just a means to an orgasmic end. He cares.

I shudder at the thought. This is Hunter. This is just sex.

Fucking out of this world sex, but nothing more.

It's just then that he hits me somewhere internally, the holy grail of all g spots and sends and explosion through me. Our eyes are locked, damn emotions fueling the orgasm that makes my body tremble and my core tighten around him.

And when my body relaxes against the bed, I see him smile. "Looks like I'm not so bad after all."

I hate him. I hate everything about him. But he's right. He isn't so bad after all. Especially not when he starts to move again, my nerve endings still on fire I swear I'm going die from the pleasure.

His hips move, his cock pushing into me in a punishing fashion, each and every thrust feels deeper and more pleasurable than the last. My hands fist the sheets while strangled cries falling from me.

"Oh fuck," he says.

Something in the sound of his voice sends me spiraling over the edge.

"Hunter," I cry out.

A moment later, he collapses on the bed next to me. He's exhausted and pleased. I am too. Except I'm the one laying here smiling like a fool with him next to me. His eyes are closed but I can still tell there is a myriad of shit running through his head right now. Like, *I just had sex with my best friends' sister, I just had sex with someone that's not Layla.* And regret. I can smell the regret oozing from his pores.

"I'm sorry," I say. And I really am. I let my aching heart, my need to somehow get back at Shane for not showing tonight, fuel my decision when deep down I knew this was right – for so many reasons.

Hunter chuckles. "I'm not." He rolls onto his side and looks at me. "We might not get along outside of a bed, but we are damn perfect in one."

It's a point that I can't argue.

The phone on the floor rings. A message dings. The phone rings again.

I reach for it, my eyes landing on the message from Shane. *I'm here. I'm sorry I'm late. Where are you?*

"Someone looking for you?" Hunter asks as he traces a finger up my inner thigh.

I glance back at him. He's still drunk. His eyes are glazed over and filled with amusement. When his fingers reach my center and part me, the amusement fades and is replaced with desire. Then heat when he reaches my entrance.

"Nope. No one."

He slides his finger inside of me and any thoughts of Shane disappear.

***

Three rounds of sex, numerous orgasms and me still lying here wondering what in the hell I should do.

Do I stay and risk an awkward conversation, or do I bolt?

A nervousness settles in my belly, a fear that when Hunter wakes and is sober, he's going to regret what happened. While I might not like the man, I sure as hell don't regret last night. And, frankly, I'm not sure if I can handle the "I'm sorry's" and "This shouldn't have happened's".

It's that reason alone I'm on my feet and heading to the door. I can't take the regret. The words from yet another man that it was fun, but no. Even if it is a man that I have no interest in.

I turn around at look back at him one last time.

We found solace in each other. That's all. That's all this was. And now, we go back to hating each other.

Chapter 6

Hunter

I take a pull of the beer in my hands pissed at myself for letting Mason convince me to come here. I should have known better.

It'll be good for you, he said. You need to quit hiding, he said.

Yet, that's all I wanted to do. Hide. From Layla and the embarrassment her betrayal made me feel. From the tabloids that labeled me a scorned lover who got in a bar fight. My pristine reputation ruined all because of Layla. The same woman that's currently hanging all over her new boyfriend, Maddox Prescott, first baseman for the Remington Rovers. Also known as the guy she was fucking in my bed.

As soon as we got here, Mason disappeared.

Now, here I am standing in the corner by myself watching the scene before me. Watching Quinn and the dozen other half-naked girls dancing all over drunk guys who are acting like they've never touched a woman before. Every one of those men are professional athletes that currently look more like damn frat boys just trying to get their dicks wet.

I hate seeing their hands on her, knowing they're touching where mine have been – where they belong. Then I hate myself even more for thinking like that. Quinn is Mason's sister. She's off limits. As I watch her dance, she catches my eye.

There's a smirk on her face as she heads my way.

"This is pathetic. You know that, right?" Quinn asks when she makes her way to me.

"What is?" I ask. I don't know why I take the bait because if there is one thing that I am certain of it's that this is going to result in an argument. She may have slept with me, but she sure as hell still doesn't like me.

"You, standing here, staring at her, pinning away for what once was."

"I'm not pinning. Nor am I staring," I reply as I take a drink of my beer.

"Sure, you're not," she says with a roll of her eyes.

I shove off the wall and face her. One look into those eyes, at that sinful body of hers and I lose my breath – and my head. I stare at her, taking her in. Her hair is pulled up on top of her head. The wild blue streaks poking out in a fashion that would normally look like a mess, but on her looks put together. The dress she is wearing, well shit, I've seen people in bathing suits with more fabric on. And just like that night in the hotel bar, and every day since, the sight of her does something to my body.

"You want to talk? Then let's talk. How long after I fell asleep did you run?"

"I didn't run, I walked. Right out the damn door."

"Why?"

"Because that's how hook-ups work, Hunter. I know you..."

"You don't know shit about me," I reply. She's always done this, thinks that she knows me, knows everything about me when she doesn't have a fucking clue. She never took the time or gave me the chance. "I know exactly how 'hook-ups' work. I just don't usually partake in them."

"Pity. You're not that bad at them... except for the whole clingy thing after."

"Not that bad?" I ask pressing forward until her back hits the wall. I set my hand next to her face and lean in close. "Based on the way you were screaming and moaning, I would say I am pretty damn good."

"And a mistake."

"Are you sure about that? Maybe I'm not the mistake. Maybe whoever didn't show on you that night was."

"You don't..."

"Know you? Oh, I know you, Quinn," I say as my fingers gently run along her cheek. "I've watched you for years, surrounding yourself with guys that treat you like shit and people who don't give a damn about you. The part that I never understood though was the why. You're beautiful, smart, and talented. You deserve so much more than you allow yourself."

Her hand presses to my chest to move me. "Move."

"No."

"Damnit, Hunter."

"Tell me something. Tell me something real. Tell me why."

"Because I'm just like her," she says before sneaking under my arm and away from me.

My eyes are glued to her as she walks away. And this time it's me wanting to start the fight. I'll be damned if I settle for that as an answer. I know I should stay away from her. Remove myself from further betraying the proverbial bro-code, but I can't.

I've always been drawn to Quinn. Trying to be her friend, trying to figure out why she hates me. And now? Fuck if I can get her out of my head after our night together. Fuck if I can't stop seeing that emotion coursing through her eyes, the pain, the hurt and I want to make it go away. I shouldn't, but I do.

"Just like who?" I ask joining her in her at the bar that Hartley set up in his kitchen. She's in the middle of doing a shot when I ask the question.

"You asked for something real. I gave it to you. Now go away." Quinn tells me as she slams down the shot glass.

"Come on, Quinn, why don't you quit hating me for five minutes and..."

"And what? Let you fuck me again?" Her words come out just as the party quiets. All eyes in the room gravitate toward us. Including Mason's.

Fuck.

Quinn, however, doesn't seem fazed. In fact, she's standing there smiling at me looking pleased with herself.

"I don't know why I even bother," I say. "And for the record, whoever 'she' is, I'm pretty sure you're a hell of a lot worse."

"Screw you, Hunter," she shouts at me.

"Already did, sweetheart," I reply before walking away.

I walk straight past Mason, Layla, and all the prying eyes of my teammates wondering what in the hell just happened. I storm out of the house, but I don't get very far before I hear my name being called. It's Mason and as much as I want to run from this argument, I know I can't.

I fucked up. The least I owe him is an explanation.

I stop in my tracks, my head hung as I wait for him to yell or tell me off or punch me. Whatever he's going to do... I deserve.

"You want to tell me what that was all about?" he asks.

"Last week... after I found Layla with... I ran into Quinn. Things got carried away and... I'm sorry, Mase. I never meant for it to happen. Hell, we don't even like each other and..."

"Relax."

Relax? Is he kidding me? He wants me relaxed so what, I fall easier when he punches me?

"It's not like you're not some random douche that she hooked up with. You're my friend, a stand-up guy. And Quinn..." Mason laughs. "I think I'm more worried about you in this situation than I am her."

"I'm not pussy whipped, if that's what you're insinuating."

"Yeah, you're not going to use that word around me anymore," Mason says with a look of disgust on his face. Disgust, amusement, but not anger. Not one damn ounce of anger. "Why didn't you just tell me?"

"And say what?" I run my hand through my hair. "Hey Mase, just wanted you to know I fucked your sister?"

Mason cringes as I say the words. "Okay, maybe not like that but... if you and Quinn..."

"No. It's not like that," I tell him despite the fact that I haven't been able to get the woman off my mind since that night.

Drunk or not, I remember every damn moment. The hurried sex, the moments when we both caught our breath and her fingers just trailed along my body. The exploratory sex. The slow sex. If I had to pick a favorite, I couldn't. Every piece of Quinn was perfection. Everything about us together was unexpected. And now, her brother is giving me permission? The plans and positions that conjure in my head are unthinkable.

"Then what's it like?"

"I don't know," I say throwing my hands in the air. Because yes, I have been thinking about Quinn a lot this past week. Whatever this draw to her I have is, it doesn't make a bit of difference, though. At the end of the day, the woman still hates me. If all these years hasn't done anything to change that. One night sure as hell isn't going to.

"You like her," Mason says with a hint of a smile.

"No. And, even if I did..." I shake my head rejecting the idea. "What happened between Quinn and I was a one-time deal. A mistake. Nothing more."

"Yeah, you're right." His words say he agrees with me, but the look in his eyes says otherwise. I would question what is going on in that warped head of his, but at that very moment I catch a glimpse of Layla and Maddox.

Looks like all those messages she left me about what a mistake it was, that she wanted me back, were all bullshit because here she is with him. In his arms, his lips on hers, just like they have been all night.

As much as I don't want to watch this unfold in front of me, as furious as I am with her, I also realize that ache in my chest that I felt the night it happened is gone. And I can't help but think it has something to do with Quinn.

"I'm going to take off," I say.

"I'll come with you. We can grab a pizza and I can kick your ass at Madden," Mason says. He's still smiling and I'm not going to lie, it makes me more than a little nervous.

"You say that and yet you've never once beat me. Not at the game... or on the field."

"Oh, hell no. Those are fight words right there, pal."

Chapter 7

Quinn

"How did I not know about this?" Claire asks.

We're still standing in the kitchen of the party. The same spot where I announced to the whole place, including every player of the Remington Red Devils, that Hunter and I had sex. And the same spot he walked away from me without another word. Without explaining why exactly he cared so damn much and felt the need to keep pushing me.

Mason stares at me for a moment. He shakes his head before walking away. And here I am being blamed again. Just like with Shane. As if it's somehow my fault and mine alone that they had sex with me.

"Not now," I tell Claire as I take a step in the opposite direction. An overwhelming feeling comes over me as people continue to stare at me. I need to get away. I need to breathe. As I try to leave the room one of the gawkers steps in front of me. He's tall, muscular, and looks familiar. I don't know his name but recognize him as one of the players on the Red Devils.

"Hey there," he says. His voice is deep, rough, intimidating.

"Excuse me, please," I tell him trying to push past him.

"Don't be upset, doll," the guy says. "Hunter might not be interested, but I am."

"Trust me. You're not."

He eyes me up and down with his slimy gaze. He gives my body a once over, no different than Hunter did that night in the hotel. Except in Hunter's eyes I saw appreciation. This guy? Nothing but hunger and something I can't quite put my finger on, but it scares me, nonetheless.

Mason steps between me and the guy. "Problem, Dunn?"

"Nope," the guy says before he walks away without so much as a glance in my direction.

"Thanks, but I could have handled that," I say to Mason.

"The way you handled Hunter?" Mason folds his arms across his chest. His eyes questioning, his face giving me a warning.

"I didn't do anything to Hunter. We just... sated a mutual need."

"Please spare me any details," Mason tells me. "I just came back to let you know I'm taking off."

"Awe, is poor Hunter embarrassed that he slummed it with me?" I ask.

Mason shakes his head. "You need to let go of whatever your issue is with him. He's not the guy you're painting him out to be. I'll see you later."

I'm drunk, I'm hurt, and if I don't leave, there's a good chance that I'll do something stupid. So, I allow my feet to carry me to the door knowing full well that Claire will follow.

"The 'she' Hunter was talking about, it was your mother, wasn't it?" she asks when she catches up to me.

I nod in response. Poor Claire has tried for years to get me to open up, to tell her about my parents, my childhood, both of the things that haunt me to this day.

"Are you ever going to tell me about it?" Her voice is soft and kind as she asks the question.

"No," I tell her, the softness of my voice matching her own. "They're my demons. Not yours."

"You're my best friend, Q, nothing is going to change that."

I press a kiss to her cheek, loving that she's reassuring me but wishing she would let it go. "I know."

"It might help, might make you feel better."

It's going to take more than crying on Claire's shoulder to fix what's broken inside of me. Years of abuse and neglect. Years of being alone and hungry with no one to rely on except ourselves. That's the life that Mason and I grew up in. Not a life like Claire's. And certainly not a life like Hunter's. The rich, spoiled shit that he is.

"It won't. But thank you."

"Want to get some coffee? My treat."

"Honestly, I just want to go home and go to bed," I whine. "Stay with me tonight?"

"In your hot, professional football player brother's fancy ass condo? Yes. Always yes."

I loop my arm with Claire's as we head out of the party to wait for our Uber. As we stand there, I see Layla, Hunters ex, and her new boyfriend. They're standing out of sight of anyone at the party and clearly involved in an argument. Seems like the happy new couple isn't so happy after all. Serves them right. I may hate Hunter, but I hate even more what Layla did to him. You don't cheat. No reason, no excuse, it is never okay. Not for the person you're cheating on. And not for the person you're cheating with. Especially if they don't know you're already involved.

When we arrive back at Mason's, he and Hunter are seated on the couch playing some stupid video game. I don't speak. I just continue straight to my room. Claire on the other hand doesn't know how to be anything but nice. If I didn't love her so much, it would be sickening. She acknowledges the guys as she passes, both of them returning her greeting despite the fact that they both seem to ignore me. I wait another moment after Claire enters my room, but nothing. I slam the door shut and sag against it.

"Now will you tell me what happened?" she asks before plopping on my bed. "Because if you don't, I'll just have to go and ask him."

"You wouldn't."

"Wanna try me?" she says with a laugh.

I recant the events from the night at the hotel to her. I explained about the guy at the bar, the short conversation, and the utter horniness that was coursing through both of us. Mix in a little alcohol and that is where bad decisions are made. I know, I've made plenty.

"What about Shane?" she asks.

I close my eyes. The picture of him that I thought was ingrained in my brain is starting to fade. As are my feelings for him.

"He didn't show that night. Not until it was too late at least. And by then..." I drop onto the bed next to her. "I don't know. I'm just over it. I don't know why I ever agreed to meet with him in the first place. He has a wife. And... I'm a lot of things, but I'm not a homewrecker."

"Do you love him?" she asks.

Maybe a part of me did, but honestly, no. I liked the thrill of being with my teacher. I liked knowing that it was a bad decision. The thing was, at least a part of it felt right. He was so much better than anyone I had dated before – kind, smart, gentle. Turns out he was also the biggest liar out of all of them, too. The others, they may have been assholes, but at least they were honest about it.

"No," I tell her. "It was just..." Just what? A game? Fun? I sigh. "I thought he was a good choice. But like every decision I make – I made the wrong one. This time, I got what I deserved."

"Quinn," Claire says, and I can hear the pity in her voice.

"I don't want your pity," I say.

"I don't pity you. It just makes me so sad to hear you think that you don't deserve happiness, that you deserve bullshit like Shane and what he did to you. You're my best friend, Q, and there isn't a damn thing that I wouldn't do for you. Including telling you the truth – even when you don't want to hear it. Whatever she did, whoever she was, it isn't you. You are sweet and kind, talented beyond belief. You just let your view of her blind you to that."

"You give me way too much credit," I say with a laugh trying to blow the conversation off because it's making me uncomfortable.

"And you don't give yourself enough."

Chapter 8

Hunter

"That is a terrible idea," I say as I run my hands through my hair.

"It's an amazing idea," Mason says. His face is lit up like a damn kid in a candy store. Of course, he thinks it's a great idea. He's not the one who would be lying. He's not the one who would be pretending.

I glance down at the wedding invitation that sits on his coffee table. The one for my brother's wedding in the Bahamas that Layla and I were supposed to attend together. Not only was she my date, but she too is standing up in the wedding. And, according to Hudson, she still is. Even better, she's bringing Maddox with her.

"How the hell would I even find someone?" I ask. And what the hell kind of person would be willing to do this?

I made the mistake of deferring to my best friend the eternal bachelor on how to handle having to watch Layla prance around with her new boyfriend for a week. I'm over her, mostly, but it's still not something that I want to have to see. It's my brother's wedding – backing out isn't an option. Seems like Layla isn't willing to back out either. In fact, I think she's actually enjoying this.

"Jesus, Hunter. You have women falling all over you all the time. Take one up on it. Besides, who the hell would pass up an all-expenses paid trip to the Bahamas?"

"So, what the hell am I supposed to do, Mase? Just ask the next random woman I see if she wants to be my fake girlfriend and come to my brother's wedding with me?" Have I really sunk this low that I'm even considering something like this?

"Oh my God, please tell me you're kidding." I groan at the sound of Quinn's voice and the amusement in it. She just had to walk in at that exact moment. I don't speak. I merely glare at her, my eyes filled with fury and desire. "You want to take some random woman with you to Hudson's wedding and have her pretend to be your girlfriend?" Her laughter is irritating. Sexy, but irritating.

As furious as I am with her and the humor she finds in my dilemma, it never fails that every time she is in the same room as me my body comes alive, my heart races, and my fucking cock stands at attention. Christ, how I wish I could hate her, but I can't. Not even after that shit she pulled at the party a couple weeks back.

"Wouldn't it be better to just call an escort service? Let the professionals handle it?" she laughs as she walks toward the kitchen.

Escort service? Actually, it doesn't sound like a bad idea. It might actually work. "What do you think?" I ask as I look at Mason.

"You're kidding, right?" he chokes out. "If someone were to find out that you used an escort service, there is no way in hell they're going to believe it was so you could find a pretend girlfriend. They're going to think you called to get laid. And your reputation would go right down the shitter. You have endorsements and your charity to think of. Don't do something stupid and fuck up your reputation because of Layla," he tells me.

He's right. The reputation that I pride myself on would go down the damn drain and fast if anyone caught wind of me so much as calling an escort service. Still, hiring someone who knows what they're doing sure as hell seems a lot easier than convincing some random woman to do it. And more importantly, it actually being believable.

"What about a friend? You do have those, besides Mason, don't you?" Quinn suggests when she returns to the living room. She plops down in the chair across from me, her legs slung over the arm rest. My eyes are immediately drawn to them and scrape over every glorious inch.

I hear Mason clear his throat, the sound snapping me out of my Quinn induced haze.

"Layla and I know all the same people. Besides, she would have heard by now if I were dating someone," I say. I shake my head. "Everyone would have."

"Unless...." Mason says.

"Unless what?" I ask.

"I am a genius. I don't know why I didn't think of this sooner. Quinn. You should take Quinn to the wedding," he suggests.

I begin to laugh, but Mason keeps a serious look on his face. He isn't kidding. "Her?"

"Me?" Quinn chimes in.

"No way, it will never work," I say.

"As much as this kills me, I have to admit, I agree with Hunter."

"Why wouldn't it? You two already had sex. Not to mention you announced it to the whole party, including Layla and Maddox. It's not that far of a stretch." Mason leans back on the couch looking rather pleased with himself.

"It's insane. No one would buy it," I argue.

"And you're assuming that I would even agree to this," Quinn pipes in.

"Really, Q?" Mason asks. He leans forward resting his elbows on his knees. "You say that as if you have a choice in the matter. Either you do it, or you tell me what happened at Columbia. Your choice."

Quinn's eyes widen. "Bahamas here I come."

"That's what I thought. Besides this will be a piece of cake," Mason says. "All you have to do is fool Layla."

"And lie to my parents. And Hudson. Fuck, there is no way Hudson is going to buy this," I reply.

My older brother may be less mature and a complete idiot, but he knows me. And he knows that despite the fact we had sex, Quinn and I don't get along. He'll see through it in a heartbeat.

"Hudson has bigger things to worry about than you – like his wedding and the woman he's going to be marrying. Besides, he's your brother. It's not like he would out you."

I glance over at Quinn, my cock twitching at the thought having to share a room with her, let alone a bed. My eyes wander up her long tan legs to where her breasts are straining against the fabric of her tank top.

How in the hell did this wedding go from bad to worse?

"You know, now that I think about it, it doesn't sound like such a terrible idea. Mason's right. Us keeping our relationship secret makes sense, it explains why none of these people you and Layla have in common knew." Quinn smiles, clearly keeping her secret hidden is more important than her having to spend a week with a man she hates.

"What about that guy?" I ask her.

"What guy?"

"Shane," I say drawing his name out. I'm hoping to piss her off enough to get her to back down.

"He's none of your concern. This is just pretend, Hunter. Don't expect any repeats of..."

Mason holds up his hands. "Stop. That's more than enough. Christ, this will be easier to sell then I thought."

"You hate me," I deadpan. "Why would you agree to do this?"

After all, this is Quinn that we're talking about. I wouldn't put it past her to agree to this just to screw me over in the end. Out me and this whole charade to Layla.

"Because Mason isn't giving me a choice. Besides, I have had to spend my whole life tolerating you. At least now I can do it in the Bahamas."

While Quinn does sound like a much better option than calling an escort service or wrangling a complete stranger into this charade, I have my concerns. One being I find it unlikely anyone will believe us and two, I'm afraid I might start to. If my never-ending thoughts of her and our night together are any indication, I might actually end of liking her.

Without any other viable options, I feel defeated. It's Quinn or no one. I can't believe what I'm about to say. Agreeing to this has to be the stupidest thing I have ever done.

"Fine," I say throwing my hands up in the air.

"Really?" Mason asks, his voice filled with surprise.

I'm just as fucking surprised. This is not me. This is not something I would do. But the idea of running into Layla and her new boyfriend has me more than a little on edge.

Quinn squeals. "I'm going to the Bahamas."

She does this little dance in her seat that causes her breasts to bounce and my body to have a reaction that it shouldn't. Christ, this trip is going to be more torture than I originally thought it would be.

"We'll need a story," I say turning my focus from Quinn's bouncing breasts and onto the task at hand. I mentally prepare a checklist of all the things we'll need to know about each other to make this work.

"A story about what?" she asks.

"Everything," I tell her. "How we met, when things changed, different..."

She holds her hand up to stop me from talking. Bringing her phone to her ear she begins to chat to the person on the other end. "I am going to the Bahamas for a week. Yep. And Hunter is my date."

Quinn bats her eyelashes at me.

Christ. What have I gotten myself into?

"Relax, man, it's going to work," Mason says. I'm sitting next to him with my head in my hands. "Besides, what's the worst that can happen? You two end up having sex?"

His laughter infuriates me.

"Not funny."

Clearly, he disagrees. "Or, who knows, maybe you two will even end up friends."

"Friends? Me and Quinn?" I start laughing. "No way in hell."

Chapter 9

Quinn

I throw my sexiest bathing suit into my suitcase.

"What are you taking that for?" Claire asks. Her eyebrows are raised and there's a smirk on her face.

"Because I'm going to the Bahamas and I'm plan on spending all of my time by the pool. Or in the ocean. Or relaxing in the sun."

Even though I'm going to have to spend time with Hunter, I'm looking forward to the trip. Lord knows I could use a little rest and relaxation after everything that went down with Shane.

"Or in Hunter's bed?"

I bust out laughing. "There is no way in hell that's happening."

She raises an eyebrow at me. "Didn't it already happen? A few times from what you've told me." She giggles at her own comment.

I did happen. And it was the best sexual experience of my life. However, that doesn't mean it's happening again.

"It was nothing more than a temporary lapse in judgment."

"Maybe," Claire says. "Or maybe it was you exhibiting good judgment for a change."

I would be pissed at her comment if it was even off base in the slightest. But she's right. I don't always make the best decisions. Hunter included. As amazing as our night together was it isn't going to change what I think of him or how I feel about him.

Mason and I grew up having to fend for ourselves. Our parents were rarely around and when they were, they sure as hell didn't bother with us. Hunter was our target, a means to an end. Nothing more than a source of food and shelter, sometimes even fun. But that's it. Hunter's family has money. A lot of it. The kind of money that you can't help but wonder if they even know what to do with all of it.

But that isn't how things worked at all. Sure, Hunter had us over. Sure, we got meals all the time and stole when we didn't.

The problem was, the fake friendship Mason forged with Hunter turned into a real one. They became real friends and bonded over football. They even made some stupid pact about making it to the NFL and playing on the same team. Both of which they succeeded at.

Then there was me. Where Mason fit in with Hunter and his family I didn't. I saw how they looked at me. Like I wasn't good enough. Like I didn't belong.

That was fine by me because I didn't need them or anyone else for that matter. The only one I needed was Mason. We were a team. We were all we had.

As we got older, Mason spent more and more time with Hunter. Their bond continued to grow leaving me on my own more often. Not only did Hunter not like me, he was stealing the only person I had. If it weren't for him, I wouldn't have been alone in that house so often. Maybe things would have been different. Maybe I would be different.

Or, maybe I need to quit reliving the past and just move on. And up. Like to the Bahamas.

"This is strictly a business deal."

"If that's the case, I would be more than happy to do business with that man any day." There is a waggle of her eyebrows. "Especially after the rave reviews you gave him."

"He is not the only man in the world capable of satisfying a woman." Though I did momentarily wonder if he was the only one capable of satisfying me. Because good heavens I have never been that satisfied before. And I'm already dreading sex with another man knowing it won't be nearly as good.

"Yeah, but... have you seen him? Really, Q, I don't get why you dislike him so much. If I were in your shoes, I would be making a go of whatever it is that happened between the two of you."

"Sex, Claire. It's called sex. That is all that happened between us. All that will."

"You're going to be sharing a bed with the man. And you don't think anything is going to happen?" She scoffs. "You're kidding yourself."

I think of his hand on my thigh. The way my body instantly softened for him. How from a mere touch, I was primed and ready to go. Then there were his lips. They set every piece of skin they touched on fire.

"It would still be nothing more than sex," I argue.

Claire's words register. Will Hunter and I be sharing a bed? The idea of it suddenly has me nervous. The idea of being close to him again, feeling his body against mine already has me getting all hot and bothered. How the hell can I share a room with him, let alone a bed?

I grab my phone and pull up his name.

"Who are you calling?" Claire inquires.

"Shhh..." I say with my finger pressed firmly against my lips to silence her.

"Yes, Quinn?" his deep voice says into the phone. There is a slight hint of irritation in it, but all I can focus on are the goosebumps it gives me.

All the more reason I need to find out the sleeping arrangements.

"Are we sharing a room?" I ask, my tone urgent and demanding.

"Uh... yes?"

"And just how exactly do you think that's going to work? I am not sharing a bed with you. And I am certainly not sleeping on the couch. Because if that is what you were thinking, you are sadly mistaken," I state.

"Are you finished?" he asks. I can hear the frustration in his voice. When I don't answer he continues "You're welcome to the bed, Quinn. I will take the couch."

My shoulders slump, the argument I conjured in my head dying on my lips. "You will? No arguments?"

"Nope."

"Why would you do that?" I ask incredulously.

There's a slight chuckle through the phone. "Because it's the right thing to do? The nice thing to do. You can think whatever you want to about me, Quinn, but I assure you my mother raised me to be a gentleman."

He sure as hell wasn't a gentleman that night in the hotel. And he definitely wasn't gentle. I squeeze my thighs together, my panties soaked at the mere memory alone.

"If you quit dating losers, you would already know that."

"You know nothing about my love life," I argue. In fact, he doesn't know anything about me at all. Nothing except how to make me scream out his name that is.

"I know that when he called you, you chose to stay with me." I can practically see him smirking through the phone.

"Go to hell, Hunter," I say as I disconnect the phone.

"What did he say?" Claire asks.

I toss the phone onto the bed. "Nothing. It doesn't matter. He's taking the couch."

I should be happy. I got what I wanted without even having to make a fuss. I return to packing, or rather throwing items into my bag in a fury.

"Still no chance? Does that mean the flush on your cheeks is from something else?" Claire laughs.

"Shut up. He just... he gets under my skin."

"If I were you, I would let him get under my skirt again instead."

He's right though, I chose to stay with him. I could have run to Shane. I could have tried to make things work. Between the sexual and emotional gratification that Hunter gave me that night though, no part of me even wanted to try. I didn't want Shane. I wanted to be with Hunter.

"He said if I quit dating losers that I would know he had no intention of sharing the bed or making me sleep on the couch." She swooned and if I wasn't so damn angry with him, I would too. It is a sweet sentiment. "Then he reminded me that when Shane called, I chose him, not Shane."

"What? You never told me Shane called," Claire exclaims.

"It was after Hunter and me... I had just been with another man. I didn't think it was a good idea to try to rekindle things with Shane at that exact moment."

"Have you reached out to Shane since?"

I shake my head. The nonverbal communication is more than enough to provide her the fuel needed for the attack.

"So, what you're telling me is that because of Hunter Adams, you passed up a chance with the man you put everything on the line for?"

"I was in a sex drugged haze. His hands were on me and... yeah, I did."

"And you don't think that means something? Anything?"

It can't. Because at the end of the day Hunter is still Hunter and I'm still me. We don't mix. We don't make sense.

So how the hell am I supposed to convince and entire island of his friends and family that we do?

Chapter 10

Quinn

"Now you want to do this?" he laughs.

His laughter jostles him, his arm brushing against mine. The slight touch sends my mind exactly where it doesn't need to be. On him. On his body. On the way they make me feel. Onto the inappropriate dreams that I've been having about him and me and a can of whip cream, among other things. This is the exact reason that every time Hunter called me over the past week suggesting that we get together so we can "get our stories straight" I ignored his calls. I mean, how hard can it be anyway?

All we have to do is smile, hang all over each other, and throw in a few kisses to make it look believable. That's when the panic set in. The realization that I am going to have to touch and kiss this man, the one who makes my toes curl, and my body quake. How the hell am I going to manage to keep this under control? Make sure that we don't cross the line again?

"We really don't know anything about each other. There are things a girlfriend knows, or at least should know."

"I agree. That's why I suggested we do this a week ago. Not on a four-hour flight."

"Do you want this to work or not?" I huff out.

"Are you... nervous?" he teases me.

"Don't be absurd. I just don't want to screw this up for you."

"Since when do you care how this works out for me? I thought you were just looking forward to the trip?" He quirks up an eyebrow, his eyes studying me.

While I might not like Hunter, he still didn't deserve what Layla did to him. No one deserves that. I've been in his shoes more times that I would like to recall. Making this woman pay is definitely my pleasure.

I cross my arms over my chest and turn my head from him. "You know what, just forget it. When no one buys this, it's on you. I tried."

"Oh, come on, I'm just teasing you."

I hate the boyish grin on his face and how it makes me want smile back at him even though he's infuriating me at the moment. "Whatever. I knew this was a mistake."

"You?" he laughs. "You knew this was a mistake? I told you and Mason this was a stupid idea. We can't even manage to be civil to each other during a flight. How we're going to manage over the course of a week is beyond me."

I sigh. "We'll manage, I promise."

The moment of softness that I offer him causes the side of his mouth curls up. "What else do you promise?"

I swat his arm. "I already told you, that isn't happening."

"It's the one thing we know we're good at."

Him teasing me this way, being suggestive and sexual, it takes me by surprise. Hunter's never really seemed this open before, this lighthearted. I have to admit, I kind of like this side of him.

As soon as I think it, I remind myself again of all the reasons why I don't like him. Then I tell myself to stay on task. "Tell me something about you that I should know."

He clears his throat and leans toward me. His voice is hushed, and I become anxious about whatever secret he's about to bestow upon me. "The number one thing you need to know is..." His eyes dart around to make sure no one is looking. "I play for the Red Devils. I'm pretty damn good too."

He returns to an upright position a broad smile on his face.

"Forget it. Just forget it," I say, but I can't stop the laughter that comes out.

He gasps. "She laughs?"

I press my lips together and shake my head trying to hide every ounce of amusement I can even though I know he's already seen it.

"Okay, how about this? I love playing football, I hate watching it. I drink my coffee black. I'm a superhero nerd. If I could trade places with anyone in the world, it would be Captain America. The character, not Chris Evans, though that wouldn't be a bad gig either."

"If you're not going to take this seriously," I begin. But when I look at him, he isn't kidding. All those things he just told me are true. "I never would have guessed."

"I'm an enigma, what can I say. What about you? What do I need to know about Quinn Ford?"

I hesitate. Part of me wants to tell him something about me, the other part of me, the part that always wins out is terrified of letting anyone in even remotely.

"I'll go with whatever you say. No one there will know the difference anyway," I tell him.

"So, you get to know all my dirty secrets, but I don't get any of yours?"

I fake a yawn and rest my head against the back of the seat. "I'm suddenly so sleepy."

"I'll get it out of you, Quinn, one way or another." Even with my eyes closed, I can feel him moving closer to me. "I know a few things you like that might make you talk."

My thighs clench at his insinuation. Christ, this man – his voice, his fingers, his everything – he knows how to play me. That might prove to be dangerous for me. Oh, so dangerous in the very best possible way.

***

I hate admitting it but am in awe of the man walking next to me. At his insistence he is carrying all of our bags into the hotel by himself. All while keeping a hand on the small of my back in a touch that feels so reverent. It's unlike anything I've experienced.

A soft "wow" falls from my lips as we enter the lobby. "This place is amazing."

"Why don't you check the place out while I get us checked in," he suggests.

I look up at him and find myself lost in his gentle eyes. Everything else seems to evaporate around us and, for a moment, I'm lost in him.

His fingers graze against my cheek as he moves to tuck a strand of hair behind my ear. "You okay?"

I nod. "Yeah. I uh... What if Layla shows up and..."?

"I can handle it. Go. Look. Explore." He gives me a quick wink before he heads to the front desk. My body instantly feels cold without Hunter's hand on me. The warmth that his touch brought me dissipated all too quickly and leaves me wanting it back again.

I shake the way too romantic sounding thought out of my head and instead take him up on his suggestion. I meander through the lobby getting lost in its opulence as I make my way toward the patio. The exquisite furniture, the beautiful décor. It's beyond extravagant and while that typically doesn't appeal to me, here it does. Somehow, they managed to take that opulence and make it welcoming at the same time. I feel at peace, at home, and I find myself in awe of all of it.

Stepping out of the resort onto the patio I look out at the expansive grounds before me, the beach filled with the cleanest, whitest sand I've ever seen beyond that the ocean, an endless blanket of pure aqua. The sun above shines down on me, a few white fluffy clouds sprinkled around it. The smell of the ocean wafts over me from the slight warm breeze. My eyes close and I revel in the moment afraid that when I open them this will all be nothing more than a dream. It's more beautiful, more serene than anything I have ever experienced. And when I open my eyes and see that it's still there, I'm blown away. I'm really here and this is really happening. I glance back to find Hunter, to make sure that he's real too. Because if anyone would have asked me a month ago if I thought that Hunter and I would be on a vacation together, let alone pretending to be lovers, I would have thought they were crazy.

But here we are.

My eyes find Hunter and I smile until I see who he's standing with. Layla and Maddox stand before him. He's holding it together but there is a faint deer in headlights look to him.

Shit.

I pull myself together and rush toward Hunter.

"There you are," Hunter says when he sees me. His words sound more relieved than anything.

"Sorry, baby," I say as I loop my arm through his and give it a squeeze. My body tingles from the touch and his must to if the way he's looking at me right now is any indication. His eyes are open with that shocked look and the corner of his mouth is curled up in a smile. "This place is just so amazing, I got lost in how gorgeous it is. I cannot wait to get into the water with you. Are we all set?"

"We are," Hunter says smiling down at me. The smile almost looks genuine and makes me smile back at him.

"Oh good, I cannot wait to get to our room and get out of these clothes," I say. I leave it at that allowing for Layla infer whatever she wants from my words.

From the corner of my eye I see Layla squirm. I keep my gaze on Hunter though. It's not just for show either. I can't help but look and try to figure out who in the hell this guy really is.

Layla clears her throat clearly not happy that Hunter's attention is on me and not her.

"Sorry about that," Hunter says. "Where are my manners? Quinn, this is Layla."

The woman standing before us is like a picture of perfection. It's no wonder Hunter was in love with her. Her body, her hair, her smile, everything about the woman is amazing. Except for the fact that she's a cheater.

"Hi Layla, it's so nice to finally meet you." The sugary sweet dripping from my voice is sickening. But she needs to know that she doesn't intimidate me, that she doesn't matter. The only thing that does matter is me and Hunter.

Ugh... I never thought I would utter those words. Even worse, I never thought that they would sound so good. So right.

"Is this a joke?" Layla asks, her eyes darting between me and Hunter.

"Why do you say that?" Hunter asks.

"What can you possibly see in her?"

Hunter scrubs his hand over his jaw. "It's funny you say that. Quinn and I were just having a conversation the other day about what in the hell I ever saw in you. Neither of us could think of a thing."

I feel a twinge of pride in Hunter. Mr. Nice Guy sure can pull out the daggers when he needs to. I snuggle in closer to Hunter. My hand coming to rest on his stomach, the feel of the six pack beneath his cotton shirt and how my tongue ran over each of the lines of it the night we spent in the hotel. I move my hand slightly wanting to continue touching him. Christ, he feels good.

"I have to say, Layla, I really am so grateful to you," I say.

"For what?" she asks with a scowl on her perfect little face.

I smile. "Because if it weren't for you, Hunter and I wouldn't be together."

That part is most definitely true. Not only wouldn't I be here with him right now, but we never would have had sex. Out of this world, mind blowing sex. The kind of sex that you wish you didn't know existed because nothing, and no one, else will ever compare to it. How am I supposed to settle for second best when I know exactly what I'm missing?

"And how is that?"

"Well, what happened was, that night you cheated on Hunter, or most likely the night he caught you cheating on him since I doubt this was a one-time thing," I begin eying her boyfriend Maddox, the star baseball player who is standing next to Layla silently through her whole jealous tirade. "Anyway, we ran into each other and started talking. We realized that we never really knew each other after all and once we did, we couldn't remember why it was we didn't get along. And the rest, is history. Isn't that right, baby?"

"Sure is."

"And I can only imagine that you jumped at the chance to eagerly lick his wounds," Layla taunts.

"No. I didn't lick his wounds, or for that matter, anything else either," I say. Though, thinking about it now, part of me wishes I had. "Anyway, what I'm trying to say is, thank you."

I press a kiss to Hunter's cheek. When I do I feel a flutter in my stomach, damn butterflies rearing their ugly heads, and I momentarily wonder if I'm coming down with something. Because having the flu would make a hell of a lot more sense than me having feelings of any kind for Hunter. But I'll be damned if when I look up at him again, the flutter doesn't reappear. Shit. This is more than some bad food or the flu. This is something crazy that I don't understand or want.

"What exactly are you thanking me for?" Layla asks, breaking me out of my thoughts.

"For being a bitch and screwing up the best thing that will ever happen to you so I could have it instead." I smile at her as I take Hunter's hand. "Speaking of having it, why don't we head to our room?" With nothing more than a wink, I lead Hunter toward the elevator.

As we stand waiting for the doors to open, Hunter leans down and whispers in my ear. "That was amazing."

"Yeah? I was worried you might be pissed."

"Pissed? Why would I be pissed?"

"I ripped into her a little and..."

"And she deserved every bit of it."

His words shock me. I know I'm here to make her jealous, but I really never pictured him to be the vindictive type. I have to admit, seeing this side of him gives me a whole new respect for him. Her eyes must still be on us because I feel his lips press against the top of my head. The moment they do, that stupid feeling in my stomach reemerges. Obviously, I'm on some sort of under-sexed hormone overload. I need to figure out some way to sate it without compromising my fake relationship with Hunter. God knows if I'm feeling like this, my vibrator alone isn't going to satisfy this itch.

He holds the door open allowing me to step into the elevator first. We're both silent as we make our way up to our floor. Through the silence my eyes can't seem to help but drift in his direction. How have I never realized how attractive he is before now? Or, more accurately, before that night at the hotel.

"You coming?" his deep voice breaks through my thoughts.

When I snap out of it, I realize the elevator door is open, and he's already stepped into the hallway. His hand is pressed against the door holding his open as he looks at me.

"Yeah, sorry." Slightly embarrassed that he might have caught me staring at him, I quickly move past him and in the direction where the sign says our room will be.

"Here we are," he says.

Hunter opens the door to the hotel room allowing me to enter first. "Wow."

"Nice, huh?"

"It's more than nice," I say as I pull open the curtains. Floor to ceiling windows lead to a gorgeous balcony. The view before us takes my breath away. The water meets the sky in what almost looks like a haze. The sand like a white glitter sparking below. "Thank you."

"What are you thanking me for?" he laughs.

"For this, for the trip, the room." I put my arms out, "The view."

"You're doing me a favor, remember? Besides, after what you did in the lobby? I should be the one thanking you."

He steps onto the balcony, his hands gripping the railing as he looks out at the ocean.

I follow him out. "For what it's worth, I really am sorry. I know what it's like and I wouldn't wish that on anyone."

"Not even me, your mortal enemy?"

"Not even you." I rest against the railing, my back to the view so I can get another look at him. "I don't get why people cheat. Honestly, I would rather have someone tell me they don't want to be with me than have them screwing around behind my back."

"I know, I don't get it either."

"I promise, Hunter, we will make this look believable. We will make her jealous and wish that she never cheated on you."

He chuckles. "I'm not trying to make her jealous."

"Then what am I doing here?"

He turns to face me, his eyes locking on mine. There's a draw, some sort of magnetic force field pulling us together. Then, just as our lips are no more than a whisper away, there is an incessant pounding on the door.

Hunter curses under his breath before exiting the balcony.

He opens the door and shakes his head at a man that is his replica. "Impeccable timing, Hud," Hunter says.

Hudson however completely ignores the disdain in his brother's voice and instead pull him in for a hug. "You're here!" Hudson shouts.

"You're drunk," Hunter laughs.

Hudson's eyes fall on me, then roam back to Hunter. "I thought I heard wrong."

"Depends on what you heard," Hunter says. He slides his hands into his pockets as Hudson makes his way over to me.

"Hey, Quinn," Hudson greets. Hayley, his soon to be wife and good friend of Layla, is standing behind him in shock. "So, you two are here together?"

"I'm standing here, aren't I?" I reply.

"I thought you two didn't get along?" Hayley interjects. Her eyes are laser focused on me, looking for any sign that Hunter and I aren't real.

I shrug. "We don't. Not always. But that just makes the whole making up thing more fun, don't you think?"

Hunter's arm comes around me. "We get along just fine. Quinn, has been an amazing friend since Layla and I broke up and well, one thing led to another."

"I bet it did," Hudson says. His smile matches Hunter's except for one small detail – mischief. Where Hunter is more reserved and collected, Hudson is, well, let's just say he's a little more carefree and wilder. A little more like me. "Promise me one thing, Quinn."

"What's that?" I ask.

"Get him to loosen up a little bit. Have a little fun."

Hunter sighs.

"Believe me... I make him plenty loose."

Hudson puts his arms around our shoulders. "This is great. This is exactly the kind of woman Hunt needs in his life. Someone fun, outgoing. Not that stick in the..." Hayley is glaring at Hudson with her arms folded across her chest. Hudson snaps his mouth shut but quickly recovers. He hands Hunter a folded piece of paper. "That's the itinerary for the trip. Enjoy your last free night. Tomorrow, the party begins."

Hudson moves toward the door wraps his arm around Hayley whose glare leaves her face for the first time since they walked in the room. They make their way down the hallway and my stomach is suddenly in knots. I definitely need to do something if I'm going to make this believable because if they're not buying it, no one else will either.

Hunter unfolds the paper that Hudson handed him and studies it for a moment. "It's going to be an interesting week," he says.

I turn to look out the floor to ceiling windows. "That's an understatement."

Chapter 11

Hunter

At first, I was pissed that Hudson interrupted the kiss I was about to share with Quinn. Now? I'm relieved.

Kissing Quinn again won't lead anywhere good. We were a one-time deal. No need to muddy the waters with some silly kiss. One that I'm certain would send a jolt straight to my dick and make him beg for her.

No, kissing Quinn is definitely a bad idea.

So, why is it that I can't take my eyes off her lips?

Quinn yanks the itinerary out of my hand pulling me from my thoughts. She scours the paper, her face falling a little more as each moment passes. I had only given it a mere glance when Hudson handed it to me, but it sure as hell looked like a full calendar to me. That means that Quinn and I are going to have to be "on" more than we expected.

"We are going to be inseparable. We won't have so much as a minute to break character."

"It'll be fine. We'll figure it out," I say.

She throws me a look before looking back down at the paper. "Tonight. That's it. All we have is tonight."

"Well, then, what do you want to do?" I ask.

"What do you mean?"

"I mean, if you're going to be stuck with me having to do all this," I say as I wave the itinerary in the air. "Then tonight is all about you. Your wish, is my command."

"Really?" she looks at me suspiciously.

"Really. I'll call Mason, we'll do a group thing, so we don't have to look so "on." How does that sound?"

She smiles and for a second, I think she might hug me. Instead, she moves toward her suitcase, searching through it for something and babbling about some outdoor bar she saw when we got here and how she wanted to try it and... then she pulls her shirt over her head. She has her back turned to me but, Christ. The sight of her still affects me.

I stare unapologetically as she slides a red satin material over her head before shimmying out of her shorts. She turns around, her arms outstretched. "What do you think?"

I'm thinking a lot of things. None of which I should vocalize if I want to keep things between us platonic. "I think I should change."

Twenty minutes later Quinn is off and running at the club with Ivy, a friend of Hudson's bride to be.

"Shouldn't you be cuddled up with Quinn somewhere for all the world to see?" Mason asks as he slides onto the open stool next to me.

"Nope," I reply. "That's why I invited your sorry ass here. I'm giving her the night off, but still have to make it look good. She earned it. We ran into Layla earlier and..." I scrub my hand over my jaw. "She almost had me believing that it's real."

"Maybe it is," Mason says

"There is nothing going on between Quinn and I," I say. I feel like a damn broken record trying to convince him.

"You sure about that?" Mason points out as he takes a sip of his beer.

"Us hooking up was a mistake. We were both in a bad place. Besides, even if I were into her..." Mason opens his mouth to speak but I cut him off, "which I'm not. There is no way in hell she's interested in me. The woman hates me. Always has."

"She doesn't even know you," Mason argues. While his point is valid, the thing is, she never wanted to. Get to know me that is. She was more than happy to tag along with Mason, eat my food, play with my toys – as long as I wasn't anywhere near her. "Besides, I'm pretty sure her having sex with you says otherwise." Mason raises an eyebrow. A moment later I watch as his face contorts into a look of disgust. "I can't believe I just said that. Or thought that. This is creeping me out."

I laugh. "And you wonder why I didn't tell you?"

"All I'm saying is that I think you and Quinn could be good together."

"How many of those have you had?" I ask, referencing the beer in his hand.

"I'm serious."

"So am I. Quinn and I..."

I hate the way that the sound of that makes me feel. Like it's a possibility. One that I want to entertain. The woman who hates me suddenly owning a piece of me.

I rest my head on the bar in front of me.

"I knew it. You do like her." The slap of Mason's hand against my back isn't what causes me to wince. It's the realization that I do in fact like Quinn. It's the only explanation for why my damn brain has been so consumed by her. "Just promise me something."

"What?" I groan.

"No matter what happens between you two..."

I glance up at him. I can see it in his eyes without him having to say another word. There are three people in this world that Mason trusts. And two of them, recently had sex and have an unspoken, unfathomable... thing. "Me and you, we are brothers, man. Nothing is going to change that."

I think back to the first time I met Mason. The tattered clothing that he wore, the paper lunch sack with nothing more than a piece of bread and an apple in it. We were ten when we met. Even then I knew that he only wanted to be my friend for one reason – he needed me to survive. From that moment on, my mom accidentally packed two sandwiches every day. Maybe threw in an extra juice box. And when he came over to play, she always sent the leftovers home with him because "Hunter won't eat them."

Quinn, well she was in just as bad of shape as Mason was, if not worse. She was thin and scrawny, her clothes torn or too small. Unlike Mason though, Quinn hated me. Regardless of what I tried to offer her or do for her, she refused to accept it. She refused to be my friend. I would toss a ball in her direction, tag her, or do anything I could think to include her. But she didn't want any part of it.

"Seriously, if you're into Quinn, I think you should make a go for it. I think you'd be good for her. And I think that she..."

"She what?" I laugh.

"I think she might be good for you, too."

I slap him on the back. "Noted." I take a sip of my beer. "Can we please talk about something besides Quinn?"

"Sure," he replies. "How are Layla and Maddox doing?"

"You're an asshole, you know that?" I say, but I still laugh. "Really trying to test that whole we're 'brothers no matter' what line, huh?"

"Always pushing the envelope, it's what I'm good at." Mason tilts his head back and drains the bottle.

I look out to the dance floor where Quinn and Ivy seem to be having a good time. A couple men approach them and while I'm not typically that guy, every fiber of my being begins to ignite with a jealous rage. The guy places his hands on Quinn's hips and sways to the music with her. She doesn't seem to mind, and that right there, infuriates me even more.

"What are you doing?" Mason calls out to me as I stride over to the dance floor. If anyone is going to have their hands on Quinn, it's damn well going to be me. I can hear the laughter in his voice.

"May I cut in?" I ask. Technically, I suppose I'm speaking to the guy, but my eyes are focused on Quinn who looks like a kid caught with her hand in the cookie jar.

"Oops," she says. If I didn't know better, I would think that she was trying to get a rise out of me.

The guy, much smaller in stature than me, releases her and steps away apologizing profusely.

I take a step forward, my hands replacing where his were and tug her against me.

"I wasn't even thinking, I'm so sorry," she says. While the apology sounds sincere, I'm not exactly sure what it is she's apologizing for.

I don't speak, just allow her words to sink in. After a moment, I realize what it is she's referring to. The charade. Her dancing with another man wouldn't look well for our "relationship."

As we move to the music, I lower my head, my lips against her ear, "I just didn't like him having his hands on you."

Her body tenses under my touch, her eyes even more filled with surprise than the night we had sex. When the song ends, when I've made a good enough show so that no other guy will dare touch her, I leave and return to my stool next to Mason.

"Nope," he says. "You don't like her at all."

"Fuck off," I tell him. I pause for a moment and decide to take a page out of his book and push the envelope. "I like Quinn as much as you like Avery."

Mason stiffens. His whole body tenses at the mere mention of his other best friend's name and the insinuation that I just made.

"Avery?" he scoffs. "You're crazy. There is nothing remotely romantic between me and Avery. We're friends, that's it. Besides, you know me. I need to focus on football. I don't have time for relationships or commitment. I just want to..."

"Play the field," we say in unison.

We both bust out laughing at his weak attempt at a play on words. The more we laugh, the more we drink and before I know it, I'm well past tipsy and, on my way, to being drunk. The last time I drank like this – I ended up in bed with Quinn.

My eyes scan to the dance floor, but she's nowhere in sight. Fuck. I stand up on unsteady feet.

"Easy there, big guy," Mason laughs.

"I have to go," I tell him. I have to find Quinn and make sure she's okay.

As I stagger out of the bar and into the hotel lobby, I can still hear Mason's laughter. After checking a few locations, I end up at our room.

When I open the door, Quinn is sitting on the bed with her legs crossed, a book in her hands, and a pair of reading glasses settled on the bridge of her nose. She looks like a cross between a naughty librarian and the innocent girl next door. I stifle the groan that my body wants to make on instinct. Seeing her sitting there like that doing things to my body that no tight dress or skimpy bathing suit could ever do.

I want to ask her why she left. Why she didn't tell me she was leaving. As I see her sitting there, looking seemingly relaxed, I already know the answer - she wanted to be alone.

"You wear glasses?" I ask.

"Only to read," she says.

"They look good on you," I tell her sincerely.

"Do they?"

I plop on the bed next to her. "Yep. And so, do those shorts."

Fucking hell, me, and my big, drunk mouth.

"You must be pretty drunk. You're doing that flirting thing again," she laughs.

"I don't have to be drunk to want to flirt with you," I tell her. "The alcohol only helps me say what I'm already thinking."

"Oh really?" She sets the book down between us. "So, what else are you thinking about, Hunter?"

"Truth?"

She nods.

"You. I haven't been able to stop thinking about you since that night."

She falls silent as she worries her bottom lip between her teeth. She doesn't want me to see it, but she's hiding the slightest hint of a smile. "You should get some sleep before you say, or do, something you'll regret."

She slides from the bed and walks toward the bathroom. "Hey, Quinn?"

"Hmm?"

"There are a lot of things I regret. Being with you isn't one of them. In fact, I think I like you a little more than I should."

Chapter 12

Quinn

I sit up in the oversized bed and look over at the hulking football player that is currently fast asleep in the most awkward position I have ever seen, on a couch that is half his size. He looks uncomfortable as hell as he lies there with his eyes closed and his body scrunched up. Yet, somehow, he still looks peaceful. Content.

I take the opportunity to study him while he sleeps. Truthfully, I just can't seem to tear my eyes away from him. The more I look, the more I see, and the more I realize that I may have misjudged him.

Oh, hell, I definitely misjudged him.

He's not this spoiled, arrogant, rich kid who looks down on everyone beneath him. If anything, he's the exact opposite. He's kind and sweet, gentle when needed, tough when he has to be. And the way he looks at me? There's no judgment there, not that I can see.

There was anger when he approached me on the dance floor, jealousy even. But the moment his hands were on me, the possessive hold on my hips, the anger dissipated.

And when he returned to the room drunk as hell, it wasn't anger or contempt or even desire that I saw in his eyes. It was compassion, reverence. The look spoke volumes about the man he is, and the person he sees me as.

And if all of that wasn't bad enough, his drunk ass told me that he likes me.

He likes, me?

Hearing him say those words stirred up emotions in me that are so foreign I don't quite understand them or where they're coming from. I'm not Layla. I'm not Hayley. I'm not the kind of girl that a man like Hunter ends up with. I'm the kind of girl he fucks in a hotel room and never speaks to again.

Except, that's part of the problem. He does speak to me. In fact, he's practically everywhere. That has to be it. It's just the lack of distance. Once we get home, once things get back to normal.... I'm sure I'll go back to hating him. Do I want that, though? Because normal, really wasn't all that great. Scratch that, normal sucked. And hating him, while easy, wasn't quite as entertaining as laughing with him is.

Frustrated with him, with myself, and with everything these past few weeks, I pick up the pillow next to me and throw it at him. It lands with a thud on his head and jolts him awake.

"What the hell, Quinn?" He groans out the words. His eyes look like slits as he wakes, like they're rejecting the sunlight streaming into the room.

"Comfy?" I ask him.

"As much as I can be on this thing they are trying to pass off as a couch." He sits up and cracks his neck and stretches.

"Being a gentleman isn't always such a great idea after all, huh?" I laugh.

He throws the pillow back at me. My hands grip the rich fabric before it hits me. "It's always a good idea, regardless of whether or not it works in my favor."

"Do you really believe that?"

"Yes," he replies.

"You could have slept in the bed," I say feeling guilty about how uncomfortable he must have been.

"No. I couldn't have."

"The idea revolts you that much?" I say with a flippant laugh. I'm not sure if I'm looking or him to validate my statement or refute it.

"Quite the opposite," he replies. I don't know why his words surprise me. They shouldn't, considering that we've had sex. He had been drunk that night. Just like he was last night when he said he liked me. "I moved to the couch because there was no way in hell if I shared a bed with you last night that I would have been able to control myself. I would much rather take my pain in the form of a stiff neck rather than a stiff...."

"Hunter!" I exclaim unable to believe the words I'm hearing fall from his lips.

"It's the truth."

"You also said you like me. Is that true then, too?"

"Thought I made that clear already?" A playful smile plays on his lips. Lips that I had been staring at and missing through our entire conversation.

"Why are you smiling like that?" I ask him suspiciously.

"A lot of reasons," he replies.

"Such as?"

"Well, because I might like you, Quinn, but I sure as hell am not about to let you get the bathroom first." Hunter bolts for the bathroom door.

The abrupt change in subject shocks me. It was as though he knew we were delving into something too deep. Something that I wasn't ready or willing to deal with at the moment.

I scramble out of bed and reach the door just as he shuts it.

My hand pounds against the door. "Don't think I won't come in there."

"Don't think I would care if you did," he laughs.

He wants to act tough. Let's just see how tough Mr. Football player is. I jiggle the handle. It's locked. "Don't care huh? Then why did you lock the door?"

"It's for your own good."

"My own good?"

"I saw how you were looking at me while we were talking. There is no way you can handle watching me shower."

He might just be right. The sight of him moments ago, bare torso, low slung shorts, it was enough to weaken even the strongest bone in me. As I move toward the mirror, I laugh at just how riled up the sight of him has me. Standing there, looking at my reflection, I contemplate how different I am from Layla. My dark wavy hair with streaks of blue is a far contrast to the pristine stick straight perfect blonde hair that Layla dons.

Is anyone really going to believe that Hunter would go from a woman that looks nothing short of being a cover model, to me?

Will anyone believe that we are a real couple when from the outside looking in, we look more like a match made in hell than anything. His boy scout to my rock-and-roll.

Hunter emerges from the bathroom with nothing more than a white bath towel wrapped around his waist. Now I know how he felt when he found me in the same state of undress at Mason's. His hair is wet and all over the place in messy spikes. I stare at him unabashedly. How can I not? He's tall, handsome, and well built. Those rippled abs, the lines on his arm outlining every inch of muscle, and that damn V that sinks into the towel. He has an infectious smile and his eyes. Those gorgeous blue eyes that are staring back at me and filled with questions. Questions probably along the lines of wondering why I am gawking at him like some pathetic high school girl.

"Sorry, I was in such a rush to beat you I forgot to grab my clothes."

"It's fine," I tell him whipping my head in the opposite direction of where he's heading. Despite the fact that he is no less dressed than he would be at the beach, the fact that it's only at towel he's wearing somehow makes the moment feel more intimate. Especially since with one false move that towel could fall to the ground and I would be in heaven.

I can feel the heat of his body behind me.

"You okay?" he asks, his breath tickling my skin.

"Yep, all good." I move and grab a few things from my bag then head into the bathroom and lock the door behind me. My heart is racing, pounding in my ears from the sight of him. "All good."

Chapter 13

Hunter

I fought the smile that wanted to break through this morning when Quinn was most definitely checking me out. But now, walking through the resort with her, her hand in mine, my smile is full blown. And it's not an act. Not part of the charade that were supposed to be putting on. It's because of the woman whose hand I'm holding.

Yes, this is Quinn, and she is hell on wheels on a good day and a total train wreck on a bad one. She hates me for no good reason other than I exist. Underneath all of that though, there is something about her. This hidden vulnerability that makes me like her more and more as I get to know her.

Not that getting to know her is an easy feat. The woman is about as tight lipped as they get. Every now and then she gives me a glimpse. When she does, I latch onto it. Trying to figure her out is both nice and frustrating. The best part of relationships is getting to know someone. The fun of exploring and learning. With Quinn, somehow, I don't think I will ever fully understand her.

Not that this is a relationship or ever will be. Despite Mason's blessing and my cock's desire to live solely inside of Quinn, the idea of the two of us is preposterous. If for no other reason than the fact that Quinn won't let me in. I don't think it's anything personal, despite the fact that she repeatedly has told me she hates me. I think that whatever happened to her as a kid, affected her more than she lets on. She's afraid to open up, afraid to really let someone in. Even Mason.

As we near the entrance to the restaurant, I glance at Quinn. She looks nervous. Before we head in there, before we make take this charade public, I need to make sure she's okay. I look down at her and ask, "Are you ready for this?"

This brunch will be our first official appearance as Hunter and Quinn "the couple." Everyone from my parents, to the bridal party, including Layla, will be here. It would be intimidating to anyone. I can only imagine how the woman who prides herself on not fitting in will feel.

Rather than answer my question, she responds with one of her own. "The question is, are you?"

When I look at her, I expect a smile, something bordering laughter, but she's serious. "Yeah, of course. All we have to do..."

"I'm not talking about us. I'm talking about Layla. Seeing her, spending time in the same vicinity as her and Maddox. That's not going to be easy." There's concern in her voice that I wouldn't expect to find there.

"I'll be fine. Besides, that's why you're here. Nothing like having a beautiful woman on your arm to keep you distracted."

"Why do you keep saying things like that?"

"Like what?" I ask.

"Like I'm beautiful?"

I'm a little confused by the question. A woman who seemingly exudes self-confidence based not only on the way she dresses, but the way she carries herself sure seems to have a hard time taking a compliment.

"Because you are? I'm sorry, Quinn, I don't get the question here. Do you have a problem with me thinking that you're beautiful? Or believing that I mean it?"

"Not now," she tells me, nodding her head to the side.

Out of the corner of my eye I catch a glimpse of Layla watching us.

"Yes, now," I tell her refusing to just drop this conversation. "Which is it?"

"Both, okay? Happy? Now, can we get..."

My hands grab her waist to stop her from walking away from me. This is too important.

"I'm far from happy," I tell her. "And it's not because of Layla. Do you really not believe that? Do you really not see how beautiful you are?"

"Beautiful isn't a word that most guys use when referring to me," she admits.

"Then they're idiots." I lean into her and press my lips to her cheek. "Because you are beautiful, Quinn. Stunning. And whoever says otherwise, doesn't deserve you." I step back and smile at her. "Now, I'm ready."

Placing my hand on the small of her back I give her a slight push to get her moving. Apparently, my compliment rendered her unable to walk. I guide her straight past Layla and onto the patio.

"Wow." It's all she says as we step out onto the beautifully decorated patio. The scene before us is beyond extravagant.

"Hayley really went all out," I say in agreement.

"If this is just brunch, I can't wait to see what the wedding is going to look like," she says.

The amazement in her voice, the stars in her eyes. It dawns on me that while I'm used to all of this, the extravagance, the pomp, and circumstance, she isn't. Despite Mason having more than enough money, neither of them has really been extravagant. Not the way my family is. Or Hayley's for that matter. So, when her body tenses next to mine, it doesn't surprise me.

I pull her in and press a kiss to her temple.

"You're going be amazing," I tell her.

"At least one of us thinks so."

My mom is sitting at a table off to the side waving us over. "Ready?"

"As ready as I'll ever be."

We head over to the table where my parents, Mason, Hudson, Hayley, and Hayley's parents are already seated. "Sorry we're late," I say. "Mom, Dad, you remember Quinn."

My mom stands and pulls Quinn in for a hug. "Of course. It's so good to see you dear."

"You too, Mrs. Adams," Quinn replies, her voice quivering with an unexpected nervousness.

I make a quick introduction of Quinn to everyone else at the table.

"Sit down so we can eat already," Hudson says.

Quinn reaches for the chair, but I stop her. "Allow me," I whisper as I pull out the chair for her.

"Thank you," she says as she sits. She looks uncomfortable, and it dawns on me that no one has probably ever done that for her. No one has ever treated her with the respect that she deserves. It's about time that somebody does. And I am more than happy to be that guy.

Her hands are folded in her lap and she's sitting so straight that looking at her is making my back hurt. I like that she's trying, I'm just not sure exactly what it is that she's trying for. Did Layla really come off as that prim and proper?

"Relax a little," I say as I press a kiss to her temple, my arm resting on the back of her chair as we wait for our meal to arrive.

"Quit kissing me." While so soft I can barely hear them, the words are a direct order. One that very much opposes the fake smile currently plastered on her face.

"Why? Because you like it?"

"Hardly," she replies. I smile because the hitch of her breath says otherwise.

Unable to resist, I snuggle in a little closer. I love the way Quinn responds to me. I like that I make her nervous. I really like that she enjoys when I kiss her even though she won't admit it. "You know, at some point, we are going to have to actually kiss. Are you going to be able to handle that?"

She scoffs at my question. "Bring it on, Adams. I can handle anything you have to dish."

"You keep on thinking that." I sit back in my chair with a smirk on my face. I know her well enough to know that she's going to argue with me. Before she can, I turn my attention to Hayley. "Quite the full agenda you've got for us, Hayls."

"I just wanted to make sure that everyone made the most of their time while they're here. Oh, and Quinn," Hayley says. "It's not on the agenda we gave Hunter, but on Thursday, us girls will be doing a spa day. You should join us."

"Oh... uh..." Quinn stutters.

"That sounds like fun, baby," I say. "I'm sure you'll have a great time. And don't worry about me, I'm sure I can find something to keep me busy."

"I can't wait," she says with a phony smile and a look in her eyes that says I am in deep shit.

Much to Quinn's satisfaction, Hayley consumes most of the conversation over lunch leaving Quinn to be able to eat and relax a bit. That is until my mother suggests that we have breakfast with them tomorrow – so they can get to know her better.

"Sounds great, mom," I say as we exit the patio. "We're looking forward to it. Aren't we, baby?"

"Yes, of course. Can't wait."

My mother presses a kiss to each of our cheeks before dashing off with Hayley and her mother to do more wedding things.

"Enjoy your afternoon to yourself kids," Hudson says. "It's the last free moment you have. It's the last free moment we all have."

"Come on Hud, I'll buy you a drink," Mason says putting his arm around my brother's shoulders.

"You're here for free," Hudson says.

"All the better for me to buy you a drink – with your money," Mason laughs as they walk away.

Quinn and I are left standing in the hotel lobby. Alone.

"So, what should we do now?" I ask.

Where she was fun and pliable earlier, Quinn seems to have reverted back to her old self. "I don't give a damn what you do. I'm going to the beach."

"I'll join you," I reply, my hand resting on her waist.

"I would prefer if you didn't. Why don't you go drink with Hudson and Mason or something?"

I scoot in closer, our bodies touching. And mine is loving every minute of it. "Because I want to be with you, baby."

"Quit calling me that."

"I'm sorry. Do you prefer honey? Or sweetheart? Maybe snookum's?"

She gives me a glare before stomping away. I have every intention of going after her because I may not be able to have her, but I sure as hell am not going to deprive myself of the opportunity to see her in a bathing suit.

Chapter 14

Quinn

That was the most awkward, most uncomfortable situation I have ever had to endure. I could feel Mrs. Adams sizing me up. Hayley kept throwing me suspicious glances. And without having to even look, I could feel the daggers that Layla was shooting at me. The whole while, Hunter sat there completely oblivious to it all.

The minute it ended, I had to get away. I needed to catch my breath and clear my head.

Because between all the awkward moments, there were his kisses and touches. The whispering in my ear. Him telling me that I was beautiful this morning. A word that no one has ever used to describe me. And it felt nice. It also made my heart race and jolts of electricity to surge through me.

What is happening to me?

Why am I even considering any of this as anything more than what it is – a charade?

I just need a minute to collect myself, to wrap my head around all of it.

"You don't deserve him, you know."

The voice, similar to the sound of nails on a chalkboard, may very well be right. But if I don't deserve him, she sure as hell doesn't either.

"Looks like that makes two of us, then," I say as I turn to face Layla. This little innocent act she's putting on is ridiculous. She cheated on him. Now she's standing here saying that I don't deserve him? "Maybe you should worry about your boyfriend and let me worry about mine."

"You don't actually think I buy this, do you?" she snorts.

"Frankly, Layla, I don't give a damn what you think," I tell her. "I'm the one here with Hunter and you're not. That's all that matters."

"He could never love someone like you," she says. Saying the words don't sting would be a lie because they do. Mostly because I know she's right. It's not that I want Hunter to love me, but the idea that someone like him, a nice guy, never would – it just solidifies what I already know. For a moment, I let his words make me forget that I am not good enough for Hunter. I never will be. "I mean, look at you."

Her laughter fills the air.

I don't need to look at me because I'm looking at her. Physically, she is the perfect match for Hunter. She's absolutely gorgeous even when she's being a complete bitch. And I am nothing like her. Not even close. While she doesn't deserve him for the things she's done, either do I. Not that I want him. But if I did...

"I'm looking," Hunter's voice says. He's only a few steps away from us. "And all I see is a beautiful woman who makes me happy." He looks at Layla and smiles. "Can't say the same about you." His gaze returns to me, his hand reaches for mine. "Let's get out of here."

"Hunter," Layla says. Her voice is commanding and demanding, and Hunter is having none of it. He's looking at me, his hand waiting for mine. Little does he know just how much I deserve what she said and what she was about to say.

This isn't about me, though. This is about him and showing this evil witch that he doesn't need her. Except suddenly, I don't feel like I was the best option here. Out of all the women in the world, why would Hunter want a mess like me?

Still, for him, I place my hand in his. And I follow him. Throwing the biggest fuck you smile in Layla's direction that I can muster.

"You okay?" Hunter asks when we're out of earshot.

"I'm fine," I say. "I'm sorry, Hunter."

"Sorry? For what?"

"No one is buying this little charade. Especially not Layla. I don't know why...."

His hand cups my cheek. "Hey. Let them believe what they want. Let's just enjoy the trip."

"The reason I'm here is to make everyone believe that we're together. And..."

"And I don't care about that anymore," he says. "If it's going to drive you crazy and make you worry unnecessarily, it's not worth it."

"Hunter..."

"Don't Hunter me. I mean it. Now, how about we head to the beach like we were going to before we got interrupted?"

I look at him like he's crazy. There's amusement in my voice. "No, I was going to the beach. You were going to go do whatever it is that men do when their alone."

There's a slight shake of his head, but I can see he's smiling. "Cute. But... You're not the boss of me. It's a free beach, I can go there too if I want."

There's this comical, playful sound to his voice that sounds so cute and so out of character, I can't help the laughter that bubbles over. I like this side of him. It makes me want to go to the beach with him and discover what else it is that I might have been wrong about.

"Come with me. Please?"

"The beach was my idea. How did this turn into you inviting me?"

"What can I say? I'm just good like that."

I roll my eyes at him for good measure. The last thing I need is for him to think that he's winning me over. I might be seeing a different side of him, maybe I'm even coming around to not hating his guts. But he doesn't need to know that... yet.

"Fine," I give in. Just for a little while. Just to appease him and enjoy the sun and sand.

He presses a kiss to my forehead. "That's my girl."

I glance around looking for signs of Layla or anyone associated with the wedding, but we're basically alone. So where did that kiss come from? Then, he laces his fingers with mine and walks us out to the beach stopping as we arrive at two lounge chairs that are secluded but still close to the water.

"How's this?" he asks.

It's the exact location I would have picked if I were alone. I just don't understand why he chose it when we should be visible. We should be showing off. "It's perfect," I say.

A staff member comes up to us offering towels, water, and sunscreen which Hunter promptly purchases. We had been so wrapped up in the moment that we came out here with nothing. Or at least, I had been wrapped up in it. It's not often I get treated by a man the way Hunter is treating me. I plan on reveling in every moment of it, even if it is only for show.

"You really are a gentleman."

"You say that like it's a bad thing," he laughs.

"No, of course not. It's just not something I'm used to," I admit. I hand him the bottle of lotion trying to deflect the question that I know is coming. "Will you put some on my back?" I swear I hear a guttural groan just before his hands meet my skin. "You okay?"

"Yep, just peachy," he groans. This time the sound is laced with frustration.

A frustration that I too feel to my core the moment his large, strong hands touch my skin. He massages the lotion in ever so slowly, taking his time and making sure he doesn't miss a single spot. As good as it feels and as much as I don't want it to end, I'm not sure how much longer either of us could manage this because the chemistry between us is undeniable and off the charts.

"I'm pretty sure I'm good," I say softly.

"Can't be too careful."

"Right. Want me to do yours?"

"What?" his eyes widen and it's the cutest damn thing I've ever seen.

"Lotion? On your back?"

"No, I'm good."

I lean back in the lounge chair and look out at the water than back at Hunter. He's still sitting forward looking out at the ocean.

"Why don't you lay back and relax?" I suggest. It is what we came here to do.

"I'm good."

That's when it dawns on me. The reason he's sitting like that and why he is refusing to let me return the favor.

"Oh. My. God." I burst out laughing. This hard problem he's having to endure causing me way too much enjoyment as is apparent by the look he's giving me. My name falls from his lips as a warning. One that I very much do not heed. "Awe, is someone having a hard day? Feeling a little... stiff?"

"You're a riot, you know that?" Even though his words tell me he wants to be pissed at me, the slight curl of his lips and the shake of his head says that he isn't.

"Don't be embarrassed, it's a hard problem to deal with. Give yourself a hand."

"Ha-ha," he laughs. "You're never going to let me live this down, are you?"

"Not a chance." I give him a sugary sweet smile before I lie back and close my eyes. The temptation to look, to see exactly what having his hands on me did to him is too strong.

Besides, I don't have much time. I'd like to get a little rest and relaxation in before I figure out how in the hell I am going to make Hunter and I a more believable couple.

Chapter 15

Hunter

"What is taking you so long?" I groan as I lean against the bathroom door.

After spending some time at the beach, and teasing me relentlessly, Quinn excused herself and ran off. I have no clue where she went or what she was up to, but the minute that she got back to the room she ran into the bathroom and hasn't come out since. The cocktail party starts in less than fifteen minutes and if she isn't out soon, we're going to be late.

"Quit rushing me," she shouts.

"It's been an hour. I don't think that's rushing you," I argue.

"Well, I think it is."

"Do you always have to be so damn argumen..." The words die on my tongue as I watch her emerge from the bathroom. Whatever I planned to say is forgotten and only one word comes to mind. "Wow."

"Wow?"

"You look..." There isn't a strong enough word to describe just how amazing she looks.

"I look what? You're making me nervous." Her hands run over the material that covers her body. The dress, so much more reserved than anything I've ever seen her in before, makes her look sexy yet elegant.

"Beautiful. You look beautiful, Quinn." My hands are dying to reach out and touch her silky skin. The small amount of it that she's showing compared to her usual attire.

"Oh. Uh..." she stammers, "are you sure? I tried to find something a little more... classy? I don't know. And I tried to get the girl at the salon to dye my hair, but she didn't have any appointments until tomorrow and..."

"Whoa, Quinn, slow down. Why... why would you want to change your hair? And as much as I love the way you look in this dress, I'm sure you would have looked amazing in whatever you already had." I take a strand of the blue in her hair and twirl it around my fingers. "Why would you change anything about yourself?"

"Let's face it Hunter, you wouldn't...

"I wouldn't what?" I ask her. My fingers brush against her cheek. There's a hitch in her breath that has me wondering, and hoping, that whatever the hell is happening between us, she feels it too.

"You wouldn't date a girl that looked like me." She says the words so matter of fact that I almost laugh. Instead, I allow my eyes to roam her body and I sure as hell don't even bother to try and hide it.

"I wouldn't be so sure about that," I tell her.

Everything about her in this moment is making me want her in ways that I shouldn't. But there is just something about her, especially now when she looks so worried and vulnerable that draws me to her. Sure, she drives me crazy. But this piece of her is doing things to me, making me think things that I shouldn't be.

"Hunter," the surprised exclamation falls from her lips.

"I might be a nice guy, Quinn," I say taking her in unabashedly one last time. "But I am not dead. And you are fucking gorgeous."

Her cheeks flush a bright red. "Th-thank you."

We stare at each other, the room around us silent. I'm drawn to her like a damn magnet. Drawn to whatever these feelings I'm having for her are. I slowly move in to kiss her, to taste those gorgeous red lips because I can't help myself. Just as I reach her lips, just as I am about to claim them, she moves.

"We're going to be late," she says. Her voice wavers as she speaks, her feet moving toward the door.

She reaches for the handle, but my hand covers hers and removes it. I'm close to her, too damn close. Yet here I am leaning in even more, my lips near her ears. "For the record, I like your hair just the way it is." A slight gasp escapes her, and I want nothing more than to take her in my arms and show her just how beautiful she is. Fuck these assholes that told her otherwise. Or didn't even bother to tell her at all. I open the door. "Ladies, first."

My hand falls to the small of her back to guide her out. I sure as hell don't need to guide her, but I definitely want to touch her. Pain in my ass or not, right now she's nothing short of breathtaking. And, lucky me, she's my date for the night. Real or not.

As we make our way to the outdoor dining area where the cocktail party is being held, I catch a glimpse of Quinn and I in the mirror. We're strikingly different but I'll be damned if we don't look good together. The visual it leaves imprinted in my mind makes me smile, wonder, and want. Stepping over the threshold and into the party, all eyes fall on us.

"Why is everyone staring?" She whispers the question through the phony smile she has plastered on her face.

"Because you look amazing. And we look even better together," I reply.

"Now I know you're lying. I'm sure we look more like a train wreck then..."

"Shut up."

Her eyes widen, a look of surprise on her face. Since we've arrived here in paradise, Quinn and I have somehow managed to co-exist. We've found a footing where we can, for the most part, get along. Now, out of the blue, I revert back to the less than witty banter that we normally partake in.

"Excuse me?" she asks, her defenses going up.

"I'm really tired of hearing you talk about yourself that way," I say.

We might be standing in the middle of a party with all eyes on us, but I don't give a damn. I can't take hearing her speak like this. Not anymore.

"Yeah, well..."

Even she can't figure out what it is she's trying to refute right now. The fact that I complimented her once again, the fact that I'm not like the guys she dates, or the fact that standing here looking at each other there is this undeniable pull for us to kiss. God, do I want to kiss her.

Our eyes lock, I beg her to challenge me, to argue what we both know is true. Quinn is way more than she gives herself credit for.

"There you are." My mother's voice breaks through our little argument. The one that has me turned on to levels unheard of.

"Hey, Mom," I say while silently cursing her under my breath for breaking this moment.

"We've been looking for you," she says as she presses a kiss to my cheek. She turns to Quinn and smiles. "I've been looking forward to chatting with you all day."

"Quinn had a little wardrobe malfunction," I lie. A guy can hope, can't he?

"All fixed though," Quinn reassures my mother and me.

"Well, good." She links her arm around Quinn's. "Come now, let's join everyone else."

Quinn glances back at me, her eyes pleading with me to save her. Maybe a little time with Mama Adams will do her some good, show her that I'm not as bad as she thinks, and either is she.

My mother leads her to wear my father and grandparents are standing. I greet my grandparents with hugs and kisses.

"Who's this lovely young lady?" my Grandfather asks as my grandmother swats him.

"Will you quit checking out these poor young girls," she scolds. "None of them want an old man looking at them."

"Oh, hush woman," he replies.

Quinn smiles. And for the first time tonight, she looks relaxed.

"Gram, Gramps, this is Quinn. My girlfriend," I say.

"About damn time you got yourself a hot little number," my Grandfather states earning him another swat from my grandmother.

"It's nice to meet you, Quinn," my grandmother says extending her hand. "I'm Joan. And please excuse my husband, Harold. He's had one too many of those Mai Tai's tonight."

Quinn takes my grandmother's hand and shakes it. "It's very nice to meet you." She then takes my grandfather's hand.

"I have not had too many. Maybe I haven't had enough. And besides, I'm just happy for my grandson. Bout time he found someone vibrant like Quinn here and not that stick in the mud he dated before."

"Speaking of..." my mother begins. "Why didn't you ever mention you were seeing anyone?" She turns to Quinn. "As I'm sure you know, we talk nearly every day."

Quinn nods and hides the smile and the urge to call me a momma's boy. It's written all over her face, I'm just the only one who can see it.

"It's new," I reply. "And unexpected."

My hand rests at her hip and I give it a little squeeze.

"Very unexpected," she squeaks out.

My mother smiles, her eyes bouncing between Quinn and I as though she's trying to size us up as a couple. I'm not sure if she's plotting our future or suspicious about our relationship. It's my mother so it could go either way. "So how did this happen? I mean, you two have known each other forever and I never got the impression that...."

"Mom," I say. "This isn't the time, or the place."

"The boy's right. It's time to dance," my grandfather chimes in. "Care to join me?" He extends his hand to Quinn who quickly takes it. Seems like the dirty old man comes off as less menacing than a prying mother.

I turn my attention back to my mother and give her a scolding look. "Do you have a problem with me and Quinn?"

"What? No. Of course not," my mother replies. "She's a beautiful young woman."

"That she is," I reply.

"She's just not exactly the kind of girl you usually go for," she comments as she watches my grandfather twirl Quinn around the dance floor. Apparently, she's steering more towards determining if our union is legit or not.

Even with the more reserved dress, it's hard to ignore that Quinn is vastly different than Layla. And I'm not just referring to the bright blue streaks that stand out in her hair. Where Layla is more subtly sexy, Quinn exudes it. There's just something about her, about the way that she carries herself. It's not just the tight clothes or the wild hair because even looking at her now everything about her has my body standing at attention and begging for more. Their differences aren't a bad thing, something I'm starting to realize more now. In fact, spending time with Quinn is almost refreshing. If we didn't argue so damn much that is. Because those moments, when we're not arguing and are just being, they are actually enjoyable.

"After what Layla did, I thought a change might be good. Besides..." My eyes are focused on Quinn, my mind on the words that Mason said last night. "I think Quinn might be exactly what I need."

My dad knocks his shoulder into mine. "Then what are you doing standing over here? You know how your grandfather is. Go get your girl."

"Don't forget," my mother calls out after me. "We're having breakfast tomorrow."

I wave my hand in the air to acknowledge her, but keep my feet headed toward Quinn. "May I cut in?"

"Sure. Steal what might be the last bit of pleasure an old man has," my grandfather says with a wink. "It's been a pleasure, Ms. Ford."

"The pleasure was all mine," Quinn replies.

Alone on the crowded dance floor I look down at Quinn. "Care to dance with me?"

"No," she replies. Her lips are pressed together in a tight thin line trying to hide a smile.

"Too bad," I tell her as I snake my arm around her. The minute I do, her body which was relaxed only moments ago, tenses. It's not the first time it's happened, but it needs to be the last. "You're going to have to quit doing that."

"Doing what?" she asks. I can already hear the fury in her voice. She's primed and ready for a fight like always.

"Tensing every time that I touch you," I say quietly.

"I do not."

"You're doing it right now...sweetie."

Out of the corner of my eye I catch Layla watching us. I don't know why she's looking or why she cares. She's the reason we're not here together like we planned to be. She's the reason we're not together period. Yet there she is, standing next to Maddox staring at me and Quinn. Glaring might be a better word. While I see her, my focus is on Quinn. How good she feels against me, how beautiful she looks when she's pissed.

"I am not," she protests. There's a fire in her eyes. I can't help but wonder if it's always been there, or if it's something new. Because if it's been there, how in the hell haven't I noticed it before? And fuck, what a turn on. I think about what she said earlier, how great our make-up sex was. Sure, it was a lie, but I can't help but think it would be even better than she alluded to. Suddenly, I want to start a fight with her just to find out.

I tighten my hold on her, my hand pressing firmly to the small of her back. My lips brush up against her ear and I can hear her breath hitch just like it did earlier. "Baby, I don't want to fight with you."

"I don't want to fight with you either...honey." Her voice is dripping with contempt and while there's a smile on her face, it screams fuck you.

The woman is beyond infuriating. Yet, I can't seem to get enough. My grandfather was right, Quinn is vibrant. So much more full of life and energy than Layla ever was. Where Layla only seemed to care about how she looked, what people thought, and what our futures held, Quinn is more of a live in the moment person. And even though she looks pissed right now, I love this moment with her.

"We should probably kiss," I suggest.

"Absolutely not."

"We're a couple, Quinn. Don't you think at some point it will look strange if we've never kissed? Besides, we're good at it. I mean, I've had better but..."

"Bullshit." She runs a finger to my chest. "I felt exactly how much you liked it."

"I wasn't exactly trying to hide it," I tell her. It's not exactly true. I tried to deny it. Part of me thinks I still should. I can't, the pull is too strong. "I like kissing you. I like making love to you even more."

She gives me a condescending laugh. "Making love? Really?"

My voice is barely above a whisper. "Sounds a little classier than I fucked your brains out, doesn't it?"

"You're assuming that's what you did."

It's my turn to laugh now. The woman orgasmed more times than I can count. "I'm not assuming anything. I know I did. I remember each and every time you screamed out my name."

"That doesn't mean..."

"Shut up, Quinn," I tell her. As much as I enjoy arguing with her, kissing her is a hell of a lot better.

I press my lips against hers in what's supposed to be a tender brushing, just a tease. It's so much more than that though. It's slow and sexy and fucking making me hard as a rock. She moans softly into the kiss, her body pressing against mine. The last thing I want to do is stop, but if I don't, God knows what we'll end up doing in the middle of this room.

Breaking our kiss, I brush my nose against hers and smile. Her eyes are wide, and her mouth forms a small O.

"You okay?" I ask her.

"That was..." She pauses.

"Yeah, it was," I agree.

Without another word, Quinn walks away and heads directly to the bar. She grabs a glass of champagne and drinks it down.

I don't even care how it looks, her rushing away from me like that, because I know exactly what it means. That kiss affected her, just like it did me. It was more than a kiss, it was more than just desire, it was filled with emotion. Feelings I know she doesn't understand. Things that she doesn't believe in. While I don't blame her, I fully intend on making a believer out of her.

For now, though, I decide to play it cool. The last thing I need to do is overwhelm her. And she already looks like she's on the damn edge as she downs a second glass of champagne.

When I reach her, I grab a drink and smile down at her. "I think I proved my point."

"You proved nothing," she protests. And... she's back.

I lean in, my forearms resting on the bar. "Why is it so hard for you to admit that you like kissing me?"

"Because I have spent the better part of my life hating you. And if I like kissing you..."

My mouth curves into a smile. "There is no if about it."

"I never knew you were so arrogant."

"Is it really arrogance though, if it's true?" I shrug.

As much as I'm enjoying this banter between us, I can see Quinn becoming flustered. The truth she let slip, the admission she almost made. For someone like Quinn who likes to keep things close to the vest, she's treading into unchartered territory by opening up to me. Even if it's about things I already knew.

"I also never knew you were such a momma's boy," she says trying to change the subject.

"There's a lot you don't know about me," I tell her. I extend my arm to her. "Shall we mingle?"

She nods in appreciation of the out I'm giving her as she places her arm through mine.

We make our way through the party; extreme caution being taken to avoid my family and their inquisitive nature at all costs. When we arrived, Quinn was noticeably nervous and now, she seems to have relaxed some. There's a slight semblance of her confidence shining through. As it should be considering the woman is wooing every person in this damn place.

At the risk of jinxing things, I think she might actually be having fun with me. We're sitting at a table with Mason, Hudson, and a few others. She's smiling and laughing, and I'm getting a kick out watching her.

"Would you like to dance?" I ask her.

"Honestly, I'm exhausted. And a little tipsy."

"Well, then," I say as I stand. "Let's get you to bed, pretty lady."

"That sounds so crazy coming from you," she laughs as I help her to her feet.

It's not so crazy, I think to myself. We've already ended up there once. And God knows I want to end up there again and again.

Quinn's been through enough shit, though. So as much as I want her, I need to decide for certain what it is that I want her for before we go any further. Is this just sex? An inexplicable attraction? Or is it more?

Breaking the silence of our long walk back to our room I tell her, "You were great tonight."

"Told you I can be convincing," she says as though the kiss we shared was nothing more than an act. If it was, then she should win a goddamn academy award.

We step into the room and I'm about to protest, call bullshit on her claim that it was just part of the show, when she grabs some stuff for her suitcase and walks into the bathroom.

"Quinn?" I call after her.

Just as she's about to close the door, she stops, her head turning toward me. "Hmm?"

I'm floored. The woman looking back at me, she's like nothing I've ever seen before and, in that moment, I know – there's something more.

"You really do look beautiful tonight."

Her cheeks flush at the compliment and then she disappears into the bathroom.

Chapter 16

Quinn

I sag against the bathroom door. Exhaustion overtaking me. Brushing my fingers against my lips, I smile at the memory of his lips being there.

Jesus, am I really thinking about Hunter like this?

Sure, yes, we had sex. And it was great. I'll give him that. But this, the flip flops in my belly, the nervous energy coursing through my veins. That's more than just sex. More than just want. With every word, every gentle touch, he makes me feel things. Things I've never felt before, things that I've only read about in fairy tales. Things that I thought were for girls that aren't like me.

And still, there they are. Front and center.

For a man that not only have I known for years, but I've hated. Did I really misjudge him? Because the man I assumed he was nothing more than rich, judgmental, and stuck-up is anything but. He's kind, and caring, and dare I even say it – fun.

The worst part of it all is, as I stand here realizing all this, there is one other certainty I can't shake.

I don't deserve him.

My past, the things I've done – he's better than that. He deserves someone more like Layla... minus the cheating.

As I step into the shower, I try to remind myself that this is all just a charade. It's fake. We're not really together. No, we're just getting swept up in the moment.

A moment that started way before this trip.

I stand under the scorching hot water letting it burn his touch off my skin in an attempt to rid me of still being able to feel it – feel him.

Then I remind myself of who I am. The home-wrecking whore. The girl that refused to do what was needed to help her and her brother survive. The girl who doesn't have one damn ounce of good in her and sure as hell doesn't deserve a guy like Hunter.

All I have to do now is gather up the courage to act like nothing happened, like he doesn't affect me. That way I can face him again. Maybe.

After my shower I take my time drying my hair, brushing my teeth, re-washing my face. Anything to avoid having to look into those blue eyes of his again.

You can do this, Quinn. I try to champion myself, but it's futile. One look at him and I'm going to be done for. One touch, and I'm his. One kiss and we'll fall into bed and sate every damn need the other has until we're drained of every ounce of energy.

And today is only day two. I still have to manage the rest of this trip.

My hand grabs the handle. I take a deep breath and blow it out. Cool. Calm. Casual.

I open the door and freeze.

Hunter is fast asleep on the couch.

Because that's what a gentleman does. And Hunter is nothing, if not a gentleman.

Chapter 17

Quinn

Hunter being fast asleep on the couch last night when I exited the bathroom was a blessing. It gave me time to relax. To get my head straight. To conjure up a plan where I can still help him and manage to maintain my distance. But thanks to Hayley's itinerary, distance doesn't seem like much of an option.

With the exception of a few hours here and there, the entire trip is basically comprised of a series of events that everyone is expected to attend.

Except for breakfast with Hunter's parents. That is solely my own personal hell to endure.

Standing at the entrance to the restaurant is a tall, elegant woman who is waving her arms and flagging us down. Dread sinks to the pit of my stomach. Not that his parents are terrible, they aren't. At least, not what I know of them. No, I'm dreading this breakfast because I already know what's coming.

"Everything okay?" Hunter asks.

"I am not prepared for this at all."

"Prepared?" he laughs. "Prepared for what?"

I shrug. "A better background story for me. Something that..."

His hand touches my arm. "Quinn, stop. Quit trying to be someone you're not."

"If you want them to believe that we're actually together, then I need to come up with something. Fast."

Hunter shakes his head. "I don't want to have breakfast with some made up version of you. I want to have breakfast with you. The real you. Flaws, perfections, and everything in between."

"You don't even have a clue what that means, or who I am."

"Then tell me. I want to know you, Quinn. The real you."

"You wouldn't like her."

"I'll be the judge of that," he says.

"So, will they." And that, right there, is the biggest problem of all, isn't it? The truth about me, who I am, where I came from? More than anything, I fear what they'll think of me. That as much as I enjoy being here with Hunter, what will he think if he knew the real me? Every awful detail.

"No one is judging you, Quinn. Not then. Not now. We're just trying to get to know you," Hunter says. *Not then. Not now.* "Please, Quinn. For me."

I don't understand what it is that he wants from me. Or why he thinks I would be willing to give him what he wants. Those emotions I got under control last night, are they that apparent in the light of day? Or, am I just that transparent? Maybe that's why this isn't working, why everyone seems so suspicious. They can see right through me.

But those blue eyes bore into my green ones and everything inside me melts. "Okay." I agree to his request. "But, if this all falls apart because you got to know the real me, then..."

The moment we reach Mrs. Adams, I smile broadly at her. "Good morning."

"Good morning, you two," she says bringing me in for a hug first and then her son. "I am so glad you could join us."

A tight smile forms on my lips as I try to keep my nerves in check. If being his fake girlfriend has me this on edge, I can't even imagine what being his real girlfriend would be like.

Not that I'm imagining that, or anything close to it.

"We have been looking forward to it as well," Hunter chimes in. "Dad's at the table already. Follow me."

"Relax, Quinn, this is going to be a piece of cake," he assures me.

Piece of cake my ass.

More like the damn Spanish Inquisition. Mrs. Adams, aka Jane, is in the middle of asking me the millionth question since we sat down, while Hunter just continues to plow away at his food. His third plate to be exact. All that food has kept him so busy that I'm not even sure he's heard any of the endless questions his mother has been asking me.

Question one million and one. "So, Quinn, what is it that you're going to school for?" Jane asks.

"I'm an art major. Photography and graphic design. I figured since both lend themselves to being freelance careers or owning my own business that I would easily be able to manage both."

Hunter's eyes lift from his plate for the first time in what feels like hours. He smiles at me and I'm not quite sure why, but his smile infuriates me. I glare at him for a moment before Jane begins to ask her next question.

"Do you have anything we would be able to see?" Jane asks.

"Oh, well, I forgot to bring my camera. Major photographer faux pas but, uh, I do have some samples on my phone." I hand over my cellphone and hope that they don't scroll too far or realize that there aren't any photos of Hunter and I on there. That would be a sure sign that we weren't together. Especially considering the pictures of Shane and I that I have. The ones I should delete but can't find the heart to.

"These are amazing," Hunter's father says as he peeks over his wife's shoulder. Mr. Adams, Peter, reaches into his coat and hands me a business card. "My friend is always looking for talented artists to come intern for him. His office is close to Remington so that shouldn't be an issue with schooling. You'd love him. Really talented guy. Just tell him I sent you."

I take the card from him and glance down at it. "Mike Flannigan? You know Mike Flannigan?" I am totally fangirling right now, the pitch of my voice getting higher and higher. "He's amazing. One of my favorite photographers ever. I... I don't know what to say."

"Say you'll call him and remind him that he owes me," Peter says with a laugh.

"I will, thank you so much for this."

Peter glances down at his phone. "Uh-oh, looks like were late for the parents shopping trip."

Hunter and I stand to stay goodbye. Jane pulls me in for a hug. She squeezes tighter than most, but it's her words that truly suck the air right out of me. "I am so glad you and Hunter found each other. I think... you two are such a sweet couple and complement each other so well. I am just so happy for you two."

I return the hug, then thank Peter again for the amazing opportunity. The minute they're gone, the smile falls from my face and I slink back into my chair.

"See, piece of cake."

I turn and glare at Hunter. "Piece of cake? Did you not hear the million questions she asked me?"

"Yeah, and?"

"And? You basically left me on my own in there with your parents while you mowed down your food. You didn't help me. You didn't..."

"Your favorite color is purple, which I found surprising considering the blue in your hair. You love dogs, hate cats. They scare you, but you're not sure why. You are an exceptionally talented artist and I am jealous as hell that my parents got to see your work and I didn't."

"What are you doing?"

"You think I left you on your own. That couldn't be further from the truth. I hung on every word you said, Quinn. And if they weren't so damn blown away by you, if I thought you needed me to, I would have stepped in. But they loved you."

"Me and this lie of ours," I say the guilt settling in.

"It's not all a lie."

I eye him curiously. "What does that mean?" He doesn't answer, he just gets up from the table and walks away. "What does that mean, Hunter?"

I chase after him, but when I catch up, he still doesn't answer my question. He just smiles at me. I smile back because I don't know what the hell that he meant by that, but I don't care either. The smile I have is uncontrollable as his arm comes around me and his lips press to the top of my head.

Chapter 18

Hunter

Quinn and I arrive to the ATV excursion site just in time. My arm is around her and she's tucked against my body. I honestly thought she would pull away, but instead she put her arm around my waist and moved closer.

The last ones to show, all eyes are on us. I wouldn't notice, or care for that matter, if it weren't for the shit-eating grin on Hudson's face, the one that tells me the drinks he and Mason went for included a little conversation about me and Quinn. Just to the left of them is Layla. It's when I look at her that I realize, something – I don't care. Not about her. Not about us. Not about anything except the woman currently in my arms.

"You sure you can handle this?" Quinn whispers as the instructor gives us directions.

"Excuse me?"

"ATV rides are fun. And you spent so long with what did your grandfather call her? A stick in the mud? That I'm not entirely sure you know what fun is."

There's a smile on her face and her eyes are focused straight ahead rather than looking at me. Smartass.

Two can play at that game.

I lean in closer. "You know damn well that I know all about having fun. I'm more than happy to show you again."

The insinuation causes Quinn to shift her body and attempt to move out of my arms. I'm not letting her go that easy. I wrap my arms around her from behind and pull her back to me.

"What are you doing?"

"Having fun," I say. My lips press against her neck.

"Torturing a woman, isn't fun."

"Is that what I'm doing, Quinn? Hmm? Is being pressed up against me torture because you can't have me?"

You would think my words were a challenge. She turns in my arms, are eyes sparkling. "Can't have you? Ha. If I wanted to, I could have you, right now."

Hell, yes, she could.

There's some grumbling like the sound of someone clearing their throat from behind us. When I glance back the guide is standing there waiting to give us our keys.

"Sorry to interrupt," the guide says as he hands me the keys.

I am too. We were just starting to have fun.

"Just a few more things to go over," he says as he gives us instruction.

When he hands the keys to me, Quinn pouts.

"You think I'm going to let you drive?" I laugh. "I have a long NFL career ahead of me beautiful, I am not letting you kill me." She bats her eyelashes subtly. "Not even when you give me those fuck me eyes."

"Oh, is that what I'm giving you?" She damn well knows that she is. Her fingers run up and down my arms. "Please, Hunter."

My resistance is wearing thin. I'm going to give into her, there's no doubt about it. But if I'm going to give in, I'm going to get something out of it first.

"You're going to have to do better than that," I say in spite of the rock hard appendage I desperately need to adjust.

Holy hell does this woman ever affect me like no other.

"Quinn?" I ask. The look on her face making me nervous and turning me on at the same time. With this woman, who knows what she'll do with the challenge I just threw her way.

Her hands reach up and grab my face pulling me down to her. My head moves, my arms wrapping around her without hesitation holding her close to me.

The moment her lips meet mine, the whole world drowns out. There is no one here except the two of us. Two people. An unlikely bond. One that I want to explore more each and every time I'm near her. If only she'll let me. Our display earns us some hoots and hollers.

"I knew you liked kissing me," I say when she pulls back. She presses another soft kiss to my lips. When she steps back, her cheeks flushed, her lips slightly swollen, I extend the keys to her.

"What are these for?"

"You win."

"Honestly? I forgot all about that."

I had too until she was out of my hold. "I'm not opposed to trying it again to see if it'll jog your memory," I tell her.

"Let's do this," she says. God how I wish there were a double meaning behind those words. A meaning that makes her mine and me hers.

She begins to head in the direction of the ATV's. I hurry up behind her, my arms grabbing around her waist and picking her up off the ground. She kicks her feet as I have her dangling in the air.

"Put me down," she says with a giggle.

"No."

She squirms in my arms trying to break free of my hold like she has a chance in hell of that. "Hunter Lucas Adams."

"Ohhh... using my middle name. I must be in trouble now."

"You have no idea. Put. Me. Down."

"Make me," I tell her.

She laughs. "You would have to put me down first."

I set her down on the ground but keep my arms around her. Just as she's about to kiss me again, a voice that I once loved the sound of, literally makes me want to revolt.

"Are you two done?" Layla asks loudly. Her hands are on her hips as she glares at us.

"If I have anything to say about it, we're just getting started," I say with my eyes locked on Quinn's.

There's a flash of uncertainty in her eyes before she agrees with me. "Damn right we are."

Quinn finishes what she started. The kiss that Layla interrupted is not something either one of us is willing to live without. This time though, it feels so natural so right. And when she pulls back and walks away? I know for certain that wherever she goes I'm willing to follow. "Ready to go?"

"Yep," I say. I'm ready for something. I'm just not sure it's an ATV ride.

We settle onto the ATV and I snake my arms around her tiny waist, my head resting on her shoulder.

"Nervous?" she asks as she revs it up.

I move the hair away from her shoulder and press a kiss there.

"Not with you."

The guide blows his whistle and we're off.

The girl of my dreams, dreams I never even knew I had, is at the helm and I'll follow her anywhere she goes.

***

"That was amazing," Quinn says as we head back to the hotel.

It really was. Not nearly as amazing as seeing Quinn relax and enjoy herself though. The woman I spent the day with today was so unlike the woman I thought she was. She didn't argue, she didn't fight. In fact, most of the day she smiled and laughed. Christ her laugh is amazing. It's not a soft giggle or the quiet held in laugh most women will do. No. Her laugh is full blown loud and happy and filled with excitement. The sound of it makes me willing to do anything just to hear it again.

"What's next on the agenda?" she asks with a roll of her eyes.

I pull the sheet from my back pocket and glance down at it. "Looks like we actually have a little time to ourselves for dinner and then there's a bonfire at seven."

"Mmm... dinner." She moans out the word and I realize I'm famished too. Just not for food anymore.

"We could grab a pizza and head back to the room," I suggest.

"That sounds perfect," she replies. "This relaxing vacation is exhausting."

By the looks of the itinerary in my hand, it's only going to get worse.

Twenty minutes later we're sitting across from each other on the bed, the box of pizza between us.

"I meant what I said earlier," I tell her as I dive into my second piece of pizza.

"Which part?" she asks.

"I am super jealous my parents got to see your work and I didn't. Will you show me some?"

"Really? Why?" She looks both confused and flustered by my interest in her.

"Yes, really. You're my girlfriend. I want to know everything about you."

She throws her napkin at me. She picks up her phone from the bed and with some hesitation, she hands it to me. "Just... be nice."

I roll my eyes at her before looking down at the screen on her phone.

Scrolling through the camera, each photo is more stunning than the last. Even the ones of the guy who I can only assume is Shane. The very man I want to punch in his smug face for whatever it is that he did to her.

"These are amazing," I tell her. "No wonder my dad wanted to offer you up for that internship. You're really talented, Quinn."

"You really think so?"

"I do." Curiosity gets the best of me when I scroll to the next picture and find her with the man in the previous ones. "Who are you with?"

I might be feeling jealous on the inside, but I do my best to sound as casual as possible about the question. I immediately second guess my intrusion knowing that she's reluctant enough to open up to me, or anyone for that matter. Asking her this question might very well undo any of the progress we have made over the past few days.

"No one," she says yanking the phone from my hand.

Since I've already jumped into the rabbit hole, I might as well continue down it. "That no one sure got you riled up."

"It's none of your business," she says rising from the bed and heading onto the patio.

"You're right, it isn't," I say when I join her. "I'm just trying to get to know you."

"He's an ex, okay? I should have deleted the pictures but..." Her voice trails off.

"He the reason you transferred to Remington?"

"Something like that."

"You know you can tell me, right? You can trust me, Quinn. I know that's hard for you..."

"You don't know a damn thing about me, Hunter."

"I'm trying. I'm trying like hell to. You just have to let me."

"I don't have to do anything." She lets out a laugh. "I can't believe I was so stupid."

I'm completely confused now. "What are you talking about?"

"I thought I was wrong about you. I thought that maybe, just maybe, you weren't just some rich jerk who thinks he can sweet talk his way into getting whatever he wants."

"What? How in the hell do you get that from me wanting to get to know you?"

She emits this growl of frustration. "None of it matters, okay? You and I, we're not a thing. Never will be. People already look at us like this must be a joke. That there is no way in hell you would date a girl like me."

"They would be wrong then," I say. She tries to push past me, but I step in front of her blocking the door. If she thinks walking away is going to stop this conversation, she's dead wrong.

"Oh please, Hunter. I am about as far from your type as you can get. Look at me." She's waving her hand around.

"I'm looking. And I don't see one thing that I dislike."

She looks stunned at my admission. "Whatever." Her tone is dismissive and once again she tries to walk away from me. I gently grab her wrist.

"I mean it. There is not one single reason that I wouldn't date you. You're a beautiful, smart, and talented woman. What more could I ask for?"

"Don't. Don't do that."

"Do what?"

I touch her cheek, but she jerks away.

"Don't act like you're interested in me. Don't act like I'm your type. I've seen your type and I am not it."

"Layla? She isn't a type, she's a girl that I dated. One that I thought I loved. But she is most certainly not a type."

"Yeah well, whatever your type is.... I'm not it."

"You aren't, or you don't want to be? Because this sounds more like you not being interested in me than the other way around. Am I not "bad" enough? Do I show you too much respect?"

"Screw you, Hunter. My life is none of your business," she asserts as she pushes past me.

"For the next week it is," I argue as I follow her back into the room.

"No, for the next week I have to smile and pretend I like you. That's it. Fake girlfriend. Free trip. End of story."

"Whether you want to admit it or not, none of this if fake anymore. But feel free to enjoy your free trip and stay the hell away from me."

I storm out of the room, the door closing with a bang behind me.

And as if things couldn't get any worse, there standing no more than five feet from me is Layla.

"I tried to warn you," she says.

Chapter 19

Quinn

"Woah, slow down, what happened?" Claire's voice says through the phone.

"Hunter, he keeps..." I stutter the words into the phone.

"He keeps what?" Claire asks. Her voice is the calming sound I need to hear to settle the nerves inside of me.

"I think he likes me, Claire. Like actually likes me."

"Okay? And what's the problem?" she asks.

What's the problem? Did she forget who we're talking about here?

"It's Hunter, Claire. That alone is enough of a problem," I yell into the phone.

"Him liking you isn't a bad thing."

That's just it, it is. It's a terrible thing. An awful thing. A thing that I want more than I'm willing to admit and am even more terrified that I may have destroyed.

"It's a problem because... because..." I try to come up with a reason and aside from repeating the fact that it's Hunter, I don't have any. No good excuses at least because the fact of the matter is – the guy is amazing. He's been kind and patient with me, and I feel like the biggest bitch for having misjudged him for so long.

"What happened?" Claire asks.

I drop my head to my hands. "I don't know what happened."

Who am I kidding? I know exactly what happened. Hunter and I were having a great day together, and I got spooked. As amazing as it all felt, it also felt surreal. It made me question myself and then I felt insecure. This new side of Hunter that I'm seeing – I don't know if I'm good enough for him.

"You got scared," Claire supplies.

I'm more than scared, I'm terrified. Not only am I having feelings, feelings I don't even comprehend, but they're for a man that I don't like. Or at least didn't. All of this on the cusp of what happened between me and Shane.

"You're right. I am. So what do I do? How do I make these feelings for him go away?" Tears sting my eyes. It's a foreign thing to me. I quit crying long ago. It seemed like nothing more than a waste of energy. The tears that I shed for my parents, for wanting a better life, they never did me any good. They never changed anything. So rather than cry, I got angry.

Just like I did with Hunter.

"Why on earth would you want to make them go away?" Claire asks in disbelief.

Because I'm scared. Because he deserves better. Because this was all just supposed to pretend and now it's real and I don't know what the hell to do about it.

"I don't know." The words come out like a petulant child whining.

"Why don't you start from the beginning," she suggests.

I proceed to recount every detail of our trip to her. His kisses, his flirting, his lack of even trying to do anything for Layla's benefit. Because I can't recall a time where he even so much as gave her a glance. For a man that wanted me here to make her jealous, he sure doesn't seem to give a damn about that anymore.

"And I don't know why. It's the sole purpose of me being here."

"Things change, Q. I mean, look at you. You hated the guy a few days ago and now you're looking at him as a possibility. After everything you've been through, that's huge."

Huge. And unexpected.

Better yet, I've already screwed it up.

"Oh, God. What do I do? How do I fix this?"

The line is silent, but only for a moment. "Why don't you try talking to him? Tell him how you feel and what's going on in that head of yours. Eventually Quinn, you have to open up to someone. And I don't think there's anyone better to do that with than Hunter. Who knows, maybe finally talking about all of it will help you heal."

Heal? Is that even possible? For so long I thought I was damaged beyond repair. It wasn't until these past few days with Hunter that I saw a glimmer of something beyond that. Something more.

Chapter 20

Hunter

I slowly make my way to the beach. After my conversation with Quinn, I don't want to be here, let alone join the group that's gathered. This whole damn trip is proving to be more of a fiasco than I had imagined it would be. That's saying a lot because I was fairly certain it was going to be an utter disaster and somehow, it's actually worse.

I sneak past everyone and grab a beer out of the cooler before I head down closer to the water.

Quinn and I had been on such a good path all day. We were having fun, getting closer, and then bam. In a matter of a moment, it was all gone. The argument we just had feeling like it had negated any progress that we made. Arguing isn't new to us, I should be used to it, but things are different know. At least they feel different. God knows I want them to be different.

This charade is feeling like anything but.

Layla hasn't even been a thought in my head. Not even when she's right in front of me, flaunting her new relationship, or trying to make me jealous with it. Whatever it is she's looking for; it's not having the desired effect. Or any affect really. Quinn has me consumed in the best and worst ways.

"Where's Quinn?" I hear Hudson as the question from behind me. A moment later he's standing at my side, a beer of his own in hand.

"She's not coming," I say.

"You two have a fight?"

We did, but I opt to lie instead. "Nah, she's just tired. It's been a long couple of days."

"You want to try again?" Hudson laughs seeing through my bullshit.

I simultaneously love and hate how well he knows me. "It's complicated," I say, not really wanting to give him much more of an answer. Though I brace myself for having to do so because Hudson is like a damn dog with a bone. He isn't going to let it go until I talk.

"Always is when it comes to women. So?"

I turn to Hudson, my brother, my confidant, my first best friend. "I couldn't come here alone. I couldn't face Layla. So, Mason came up with this stupid idea. I was going to call a..." I groan, unable to believe I am actually going to admit this to him. "I was going to call an escort service, but Mason convinced Quinn. Now, here we are."

"And when did you start liking your pretend girlfriend?

I run my hand through my hair. "I would like to say it started when we got here."

"But?" Hudson laughs.

"It might have started the night we had sex."

Hudson can't even contain his laughter at this point. "Why is it so hard for you to admit?"

"Because it feels like a lost fucking cause. No matter what I do or how much I want it, we're not going to work."

I think about all the laughing on the ATV. The fun little race to the bathroom this morning. Then, like a switch, it all flipped. And that's why I'm out here though, isn't it? Because hearing her say that it was pretend, that I was nothing more than a means to an end hurt worse than finding Layla with another man in my own bed?

"I wouldn't be so sure if I were you." He nods behind me. "Looks like she isn't so tired after all."

My eyes flick over to the edge of the beach. Quinn is standing there, the short blue dress she's wearing blowing ever so slightly in the wind. She looks uncomfortable and out of place as her eyes scan the crowd. And stunning. So absolutely stunning.

"When I heard you showed up with Quinn, I knew it was bullshit," Hudson tells me. "It's no secret you two weren't exactly friends, or hell, even amicable. Then, when I saw the two of you together, I knew instantly that it wasn't. I saw that look in your eyes. Hers, too."

"Oh yeah?" I chuckle. "And what look is that?"

"Confusion," he laughs. "I remember it damn well. It's exactly how I felt when I met Hayley."

"So, because you're getting married, you think you're the love expert now?"

Hudson throws his head back and laughs. "Expert? Hell no. I'm lucky that Hayls hasn't kicked me to the curb yet. What I do know is that we don't get to pick who we want to be with." Hudson runs his hand through his hair. "You think in a million years I would have thought I would have ended up with a girl like Hayley? She's responsible, detail-oriented, and serious. And yet, I can't imagine my life without her."

I nod, understanding the words more than he realizes. No, Quinn isn't exactly the kind of woman that I envisioned myself ending up with. Having spent time with her though... the idea of not having her in my bothers me. I like her. I like who I am when I'm with her.

"Go," Hudson tells me. He gives me a slight shove in her direction.

Quinn gives me a small, unsure smile when I reach her. She looks almost scared, but I'm not sure if it's of me or of what she's feeling. Whatever that might be.

"I'm glad you came," I tell her.

"I'm sorry, Hunter. I didn't mean what I said."

"I'm sorry, too. I didn't mean to push."

"You didn't. I just..."

I press my finger to her lips to silence her. "Come for a walk with me."

Quinn glances to the right where Layla is standing watching us. "Yeah, of course, baby."

I shake my head. "Drop the act, Quinn. This isn't about Layla. This is about us."

"Us?" her voice is unsteady as she says the word.

"Yeah, us," I say with a smile as I tuck a strand of hair behind her ear. "What do you say?"

"What about the bonfire?" she asks.

I lean in closer. "They don't even have s'mores," I tell her. The dissatisfaction in my voice more than evident, but for good measure I throw in an exaggerated eye roll.

She gasps. "No s'mores? What is wrong with those two?"

"Right?" I say laughing. "Nothing better than a cold beer and a warm s'more."

"That's gross, Hunter. Beer and s'mores?" She makes a face to show her disgust with my suggestion.

"Don't knock it until you've tried it."

I extend my hand to her. Her eyes look at it for a moment, then flutter back up to meet my gaze. "Are you sure?"

The hesitancy in her eyes matches my own, I'm sure. But for some reason, when she poses the question to me, it disappears. For me at least.

I grab her hand and tug her against me. "I've never been more sure of anything, Quinn."

With our fingers laced together, I grab a blanket from the pile with my other hand.

"What's the blanket for?" she asks.

I shrug. "Just in case we wanted to sit and talk. Or..."

"Or, what?"

"Kiss."

"Kiss, huh? You think I want to kiss you?"

"Yep. Know what else I think?"

"Hmm?"

"I think that I'm starting to like this whole getting along with you thing. And that maybe, just maybe, you might too."

She lets out a soft laugh before she forces her face to return to a more serious nature. "And that's why you think I want to kiss you?"

"Oh, no. I already know you want to kiss me. It's why I think you like me. Like, really like me."

Her laughter fills the air. It's the sweetest, most carefree sound I've ever heard, and I only wish that she made it more. Even as she laughs though, even though her eyes have the slightest twinkle to them, I can still see the sadness and pain lurking behind them. While she might tell herself, it has to do with Shane, I think it's something so much deeper.

It's the past that she refuses to acknowledge. The horrific childhood she pretends to forget that still haunts her. Maybe to some guys that kind of baggage, the shit storm that I already know it's going to cause if we make a real go of this, it's a reason to walk away. To me, though, it only fuels my desire for her. If nothing else, it makes me want to be the one to help her make it go away. Not because I have some bullshit hero complex, but because I want to be the man that's there for her. For everything. Every smile. Every tear. Every moment good and bad.

"Now you're talking crazy. How much have you had to drink?"

"This isn't some alcohol induced admission, Quinn. This is real."

I lay the blanket down on the sand and sit. She stands there, looking down at me, her eyes filled with questions. I grab her hand and tug just hard enough to knock her off balance.

"Hey," she shouts as she falls into me.

She might be yelling at me, but she's smiling while she does it. I'm smiling too because she's in my arms and I have no intention of letting go.

I turn to face her. She's sitting there, in the sand, the moonlight cascading over her making her look even more soft and vulnerable than I know she is right now. "I want you, Quinn. The real you."

"Why?"

Against my better judgment, I allow my hands to come to rest on her silky thighs. I pause for a moment trying to control my desire for her while debating whether I want to go through with this or not.

"Hell if I know," I say with a slight laugh. "What I do know is that I expected to come here and see Layla with Maddox and to be devastated – to struggle. But I haven't. Not once. And there's only one reason for that."

"And... I'm that reason?"

I nod. "Honestly, Quinn, I haven't really thought about Layla since..."

"We hooked up?"

"It was more than that, but... yeah. Something between us changed that night. You can't tell me you don't feel it."

She's silent for a moment, letting my words sink in. Or, at least, that's what I hope she's doing. After all, this is Quinn and what she's thinking, or feeling is a mystery to me. It pains me to think that words like that have never been spoken to her. The astonishment in her eyes as I said them fueling my knowledge.

"I don't know what to say." Not the words I want to hear, but at least she's being truthful with me.

"You don't have to say anything."

My hands come up to her face, cupping her cheeks. "What are you doing?" she asks.

"Actions speak louder than words," I tell her as my lips meet hers in a seductive kiss.

Not just any kiss. Not by a long shot. Not when every piece of me has been dying to taste her again since that night on the dance floor. When she doesn't push me away, I move my hand behind her head and thread my fingers through her hair. I am not ready for this to end. Thank fuck she doesn't seem to be either. Her lips part and I take the opportunity to deepen the kiss. Her hands fist my shirt, her body presses against mine, and just like that I am lost in the whirlwind that is Quinn.

When she pulls back her lips are swollen, and she is breathless. Her fingers touch the place where mine just left. "What was that?"

"A kiss."

"That wasn't just a kiss. That was..."

What Quinn? I silently implore her. She's right that wasn't just a kiss. That was just the beginning of so much more. I just need to know that she feels it, too. An acknowledgement, that's all I need before I let myself get too carried away. Fall too deeply for her.

She wraps her arms around my neck, and she pulls me in for a kiss.

Actions speak louder than words.

The way she is kissing me speaks volumes right now. I can actually feel the emotion she's pouring into it. I feel her doing the same as me – losing myself in us. My hands splay across her ass and pull her against me. I'm rock hard and dying to be inside her. I lie back on the blanket with her on top of me making sure not to break our kiss. I refuse to let this moment end. Nothing has ever felt or tasted as good as Quinn Ford.

"Hunter," she says in a breathy voice that makes my balls tighten.

"Christ, Quinn," I say between the kisses I am trailing down her neck.

"We shouldn't..."

"Stop? No, we shouldn't."

Her hips press against me to meet the erection that is straining against my khaki shorts as she sits astride me. Her hands are pressed to her chest. She's looking at me bewildered, wild, and awestruck and I feel the same damn way.

I never would have guessed that Quinn, of all people, would be the woman who grabs me by the balls and makes me fall for her.

Certainly not this hard or this fast. That's exactly what I've done these past few days, though - I've fallen for her.

I lie there on the blanket, my eyes glued to her as she begins to tug the fabric of her dress up. Then over her head. I quickly sit, my body pressing against her to keep her sheltered. "What the hell are you doing?"

"Going for a swim," she says. "I think we both need to cool off."

She slides out of my arms and walks toward the water. Her body stepping away from mine cools me off plenty and all I can think about is having the heat of her body in my arms in again. Every step she takes backwards she discards something – her shoes, her bra, that lace thong that slides down her sexy thighs and falls into the sand. I watch her intensely as she stands there, completely naked and uninhibited staring at me.

It's such a turn on and a far cry from what she looked like less than twenty minutes ago. The biggest change, the thing that intrigues me the most, is the mischief I see in her eyes. It's clear as day despite the dim light of the moon.

"Are you going to come or not?" She says the words as a challenge, one that I am more than happy to accept. Mix that in with the look she's giving me, come hither mixed with trouble, and I scramble to my feet.

Quinn Ford is the type of woman to make you do stupid things.

Like stripping off all your clothes and following her into the ocean.

Chapter 21

Quinn

"Are you going to come? Or not?" The seductive words fall from my lips without my permission.

This little plan of mine was spur of the moment, a desperate attempt to put some space between us. Sure, we've kissed before. We've even had sex. But that? None of it holds a candle to what we just shared. There was so much emotion in that kiss, so much being said. Every bit of it terrifying me and exhilarating me at the same time.

The experience was so new to me, the emotion behind it so raw, that I had to get away. I needed distance to regain my footing. So, I shoved off him and stood before him completely naked begging him with my body and my eyes to join me, to be with me.

I challenged him, dared him to come to me.

He stands from the blanket – challenge accepted.

What the hell am I going to do with him once he's here? I'm not sure if I can handle him kissing me again. If he does, I might never stop.

I watch as he stands discarding his clothes before moving in my direction. My eyes study his body, every square inch of muscled perfect, every hardened ounce. My tongue darts out to wet my lips in appreciation of the handsome man headed toward me.

His bright blue eyes darken with desire more and more with every step that he takes.

When he reaches me, the look of desire is still in his eyes, but there's a playful smile on his lips. His strong arms snake around me and I feel at ease – safe. Then the corner of his mouth quirks up, his eyes flicker, and his strong arms hoist me up and set me on his shoulder.

"Hunter," I squeal.

No sooner does the sound escape me, we hit the chilled water. Goosebumps cover every inch of my body and I can't tell if it's from the water, or him.

"Cooled off enough?" he says with a laugh.

The guy I am used to seeing so serious and so in control looks relaxed and happy and dare I say – fun? I splash him, he splashes back. He reaches for me and I shove him away. We play like little kids in the gorgeous ocean water, laughing and carefree.

Then his hand captures my wrist, tugging me to him. He doesn't speak, only smiles before his lips capture mine again. I swear the world stops spinning. Everything around us is silent and serene and we are the only two people that exist in the world.

"What am I going to do with you?" he asks.

Our bodies are pressed together, his excitement more than evident. "I know what you want to do."

His laughter floats through the air. It's a sound like I've never heard from him before, he is like I've never seen him before.

"Where has this Hunter been all my life?" I ask.

His eyes drop down to where my chest is against his. "Waiting for you, I guess." He clears his throat almost as if he's uncertain of the words that he is going to say. "I meant what I said earlier."

"Which part?" I know what he's referring too but I need to hear him say it again. I need the confirmation because the pieces of me that are broken refuse to believe it's possible. It may have taken that kiss to make me realize it, but I think I might just like him too.

He knows I need to hear it. That I need to feel it. Our bodies are entwined, his lips next to my ear. "I like you, Quinn. I really, really like you."

The words send a shiver down my spine. I want to ask him to say it again. I want to hear it over and over until I believe that someone like him could actually want someone like me. More than anything I want to believe it. I want to be his.

Although the admission is internal, it still startles me.

I want Hunter Adams.

Maybe I always have.

Maybe it's not him that didn't think I was good enough. Maybe, it was me. Those thoughts, deflecting my own insecurities onto believing it's how he thought of me have kept me from finding this. Not anymore.

Claire told me to be honest with him.

"I like you, too," I whisper. It's the truth. A start. All the bad things, the pieces of me I don't want anyone to see, those can come later. Not now. Not when we're in the middle of something so perfect.

"What do you think we should do about this mutual like we have of each other?"

His fingers slide down my body, between my thighs, and straight to...

"Jesus, Quinn, can't you ever keep your clothes on?" a female voice calls out.

Hunter's head whips in the direction of the beach where Layla stands with all of our clothes and the blanket in her hands.

"Put it down," Hunter orders her.

"Not a chance in hell," she laughs as she begins to walk away.

"Damnit, Layla." He says the words like a scolding. One she doesn't seem to give a damn about. If my instincts were right and she really is still in love with him, this isn't something she would want to do. Unless, of course, she hates me more. Since she doesn't seem to be backing down, I'm guessing the latter is correct.

Hunter wades through the water, stepping out to go after her, but she's gotten too far. Or at least too far for him to go in his current state – naked, dripping wet, and sexy as sin.

I sit in the water not really sure what to do, or how to get us out of this mess that I got us into.

"I am so sorry," I tell him.

"For what?"

"This," I say, as I make my way out of the water and wrap my arms around myself. "It was a terrible idea. Typical Quinn doing stupid shit."

"Woah...no. This was a great idea. I have had more fun tonight than I have had in a long time."

"Really? Even though we're naked and stranded now?"

"Maybe even more because of it." When he smiles at me, I swear my heart skips a beat.

I glance around the empty beach trying to develop some sort of escape strategy. My eyes fall on one lone piece of clothing that was left behind and my laugh is instantaneous.

"What's so funny?"

I squat down and pick up the item and dangle it in front of him. "A sock. Looks like you can cover up after all."

I don't know what it is or why I find it so funny, but I am laughing so hard that my stomach begins to hurt. And when he joins in, it's solidified that this right here is my all-time favorite moment of my life.

"So, now what?" I ask.

Our laughter dies down and the look on his face grows serious. "We need to get you covered and find a way to get back in our room."

I sashay past him. "I don't need to be covered; I have nothing to be embarrassed about."

"No, you definitely do not," he agrees. "But..."

"But what?"

His jaw ticks as he takes me in. I swear my body sizzles just from the way he looks at me. "I... uh..."

"We're standing here staring at each other naked. Pretty sure there's nothing we can't share at this point."

He rubs his hand along his jaw. "I don't want people looking at you."

It's possessive and sweet and screams at what a gentleman he really is. He would rather be out there for everyone to look at that let anyone catch a glimpse of me.

"I will head back to the hotel, get you some clothes, and then..." he begins.

"That's sweet, but you're the high-profile football player with a reputation to protect. I'll do it."

"No way."

"Either I go, or we're in this together. Your choice, tough guy?"

He sighs and shakes his head. "Fine. But if we're doing this, you need to follow my lead."

"Yes, sir," I say as I salute him.

He stands us so his back is facing my front. My arms are around his waist and I'm in just the right position to grab what I desperately want to take. Layla could have at least left the blanket. Had she, there's no doubt I would be on my back, Hunter's body over me, screaming out his name in pleasure even more profusely than I did in the hotel that night.

That night was a fluke. This. This is real.

My hand reaches, taking him in my hand.

"Oh fuck, Quinn." He allows my hand to stroke him a few times before tearing it away. He turns to me, his fingers under my chin. "You're going to make me cum in your hand."

"Got somewhere else you would prefer?" I taunt him.

He emits a low growl. "I can think of a few."

"A few?" I ask my eyes wide.

All Hunter does is wink before turning me around. This time it's his front to my back and his big bulky arm covering my breasts. Something hard presses against my back and makes me giggle.

"Sorry."

"I'm not." If anything, I'm more turned on than before. Anticipating what is undoubtedly going to happen when we get back to our room.

His strong muscular arm wraps around the front of me covering my breasts.

"This okay?" he asks.

"Sure. But you know...you can just touch them if you want. You don't have to pretend to cover them."

"You can cover your uh..."

"Really?" I laugh. "You can't say it?"

"Just do it."

"Say it," I taunt him. He lets out a breath. "Say... pussy."

"There are way better things for me to do with my mouth than say the word."

"Say it."

His voice gets low and deep. "Cover your pussy, Quinn. Because if anyone else looks at it, I won't be tasting it tonight. And you do want me to taste you, don't you?"

His words are so unexpected that I'm not sure what to do except allow the moan it instills to fall from my lips. Who knew that mister nice guy over here had such a dirty, sexy mouth? Every ounce of restraint is used to not touch myself or beg him to touch me.

"Yes or no, Quinn?"

"Yes."

"Good. Now, move."

We slowly shimmy back toward the resort, trying to keep our laughter to a minimum so as not to attract attention. As if there is a chance in hell that a six-foot four, naked football player isn't going to attract any attention. Especially when he has his arms around a very naked girl with blue streaks in her hair.

"It keeps poking me," I giggle.

"It's in that condition because of you, so you're going to have to deal with it."

"I thought you were going to say take care of it," I say.

"We'll get to that... later." He moves us behind a tall bush near the pool. "You stay here. I'm going to grab that towel."

"We need more than one," I remind him.

"Yeah, well, let's take what we can get."

With stealth vibes the hulking football player steals a towel and dashes behind the bush.

"Woo-hoo," I call out throwing my hands in the air. My entire body on display for him.

He takes me in for a moment, his eyes scraping over my body, his hands clenching the towel, itching to touch me. A nearby sound interrupts him and within a second the towel is wrapped around me covering me up.

"What are you doing?" I giggle.

"Covering you up."

"What about you?" I glance down at his still visible and uncomfortable looking erection then back up to his smiling face.

"I'm good. Let's go."

I snuggle back up against him to cover him up. "That's not helping."

"I wasn't trying to help."

Somehow, we skate through the hotel without being noticed, or at least no one acts like they notice. Again, how can they not? We look crazy, ridiculous, and stealthy mission impossible movements have both of us laughing despite the desire coursing through our veins.

We're almost there. Almost to the front desk where we need to go to get a new room key.

"I'll go," I tell him as we stand there looking at the concierge.

"No." His voice is deep, solid, and completely unwavering in his decision.

"At least take the towel," I say as I begin to undo it.

His hand comes up and covers mine. "Don't."

Sweet as it is, it's also insane. There is no reason that my covered body shouldn't be the one to go to the front desk. Or that he couldn't use the towel while I hide here in the hall. Either option is viable, but he doesn't seem to be willing to give into any of them.

"Hunter, you're being..."

"Hunter? Quinn?" a voice says.

I freeze when I see Mrs. Adams standing in front of us. I can feel the heat of embarrassment on my cheeks and the desire to run in my feet.

Great. Sure. Of course.

This morning the woman loved me. Now she's going to think I'm nothing but some slut trying to bed her baby boy. Not that she would be completely wrong.

My gaze drops to the floor. I refuse to look at her, to meet her eyes to see the disapproval that I am certain is in them.

"What are you two... up to?" she asks.

Dread sinks further into the pit of my stomach. But I hear her stifle a laugh and can't help but look up. Where I expect to find anger or disappointment in her eyes, there is amusement. Is she really not angry? Does she not hate me for something I am sure she knows is my fault since there is no way in hell Hunter, the good version of him, the one I seem to be infiltrating at least slightly, would do this.

"Very funny, mom," Hunter says. "We went for a swim and Layla stole our clothes. Think you could, uh... help us out maybe?"

"I don't know. Looks like you're handling things," she laughs.

"Mom."

"Okay, okay, I'll be right back."

With the towel tucked under my arms, I turn toward the wall and rest my head against it. "Oh my God. Of all the people we could have run into, it had to be your mother?" I hear him laugh. "It's not funny."

"I thought I was the one that wasn't any fun."

"Hunter," I scold him.

"Relax, okay. It's not exactly the first time that my mom has caught me in a compromising position."

His admission shocks me. I turn and face him needing to seek out if he's being honest with me, or just trying to make me feel better. "Are you serious?"

"Yes, and I will tell you all about it later, but for now, please just relax."

"Here," Mrs. Adams says as she hands us some clothing. "You're lucky the gift shop was open."

"Yeah, really lucky," Hunter laughs as he steps into the flowered shorts that his mother got him.

I slide the less tacky dress she got me over my head before letting the towel drop to the floor. "Thank you."

"You're welcome dear."

Hunter excuses himself to head to the front desk to get a room key.

"I'm glad you two are enjoying yourselves," his mom tells me.

"We are. I am so sorry about..."

She waves her hand at me. "Enjoy your evening." She gives my hand a squeeze before heading off.

A minute later Hunter returns with a room key and we make our way back to our room. Stopping in front of the door there, on the floor, lie our clothes. "That bitch," I say with a shiver.

"You're cold," Hunter says running his hands up and down my arms.

"I'm fine," I lie. It wasn't until just now that I realized how cold I was. The water, the cool breeze on the beach, followed by the air conditioning in the hotel lead me to uncontrollable shivers.

He opens the door and lets us into the room then disappears into the bathroom. When he comes back out, he tells me, "The shower is running, go warm up."

"You don't want to join me?" I say through my chattering teeth.

I'm cold. Freezing. But there is one thing that I am sure will warm me up more and faster than a damn hot shower. And that is Hunter's hands on me.

Chapter 22

Hunter

Not want to join her?

Is that even a real question?

There is nothing that I want more.

Without another word, I slide the shorts my mom had provided only a few moments ago, to the ground and step out of them. She's standing before me, shivering.

"Here, this might help," I tell her.

My hands grip the flimsy material of her dress and pull it up and over her head. If she weren't so cold, I would stare at her forever. A little wild, a little sweet, a whole lot of sexy stands before me and I can't take my eyes off her.

I lift her from the ground, her petite body floating into my arms like nothing. Her legs wrap around my waist as I step us into the shower. The warm water cascading over us isn't what heats me. It's her. It's the look in her eyes. The simultaneous shadow of thrill, desire, and fear. She takes my breath away and I hate that I never noticed all of this about her before now.

Right now, she is nothing more than woman. A beautiful, vulnerable woman who is opening herself up to me. Not just physically, but emotionally. I can see it etched on her face. Whatever is happening between us – it matters. It's more than just sex.

My lips capture hers unable to resist the pull any longer. I taste her, I take her, I fucking brand her and make her mine. Because that's exactly what I want her to be. Mine.

The sound of my name falling from her lips, the soft moan as I press her against the wall, my mouth trailing down her neck.

"All you have to do is say the word and I will stop."

Please, God, don't let her say it. Don't let her tell me to stop.

"Don't stop, Hunter. Whatever you do, don't stop."

Her body shivers, her nipple pebbles beneath my tongue. It's not the cold that's causing it anymore. No, she's nice and warm now. It's me. It's us.

"Please, Hunter."

Jesus.

"Please what?" I growl, my teeth tugging gently tugging on her nipple as I massage her other breast with my hand.

I set her back on her feet as I dip to my knees.

"What are you doing?" she asks, her fingers threading through my hair as I kneel before her.

"I promised you I would taste you." My lips brush against her stomach. "I never make a promise I don't intend on keeping."

"Hunter, you..." A swipe of my tongue down her stomach to the seam of her inner thigh. "Oh, God." Her legs are parted, her hands up pressed flat against the wall and she moves her leg onto my shoulder.

My fingers find her center, the slickness there is pure arousal and has nothing to do with the water that is falling over us. I coat my fingers in her then bring them to my mouth. "So good."

I dip my head, tasting and taunting her. She grinds against me, her body begging and pleading for more as her moans get louder and louder. Every inch of her perfection, every sound a blissful rhythm.

"Yes. Right there. Holy shit."

I feel her tighten, her body filling with pleasure as her orgasm hits her. Her body tenses, then sags against the wall. My tongue takes one last taste of her in pure satisfaction.

I turn off the water and hand her a towel. "Are you warm now?"

"On fire," she replies. Wrapped in the plush fabric she steps into me. "Please tell me you're not done with me yet."

"Not even close."

With her hand in mine I lead her to the bed. "Bend over."

Her mouth falls open; surprise written all over her gorgeous face. The demand in my instruction – the force I say it with has her stunned silent. She takes her bottom lip between her teeth and studies me for a moment. "Excuse me?"

I don't have the power to wait any longer. My hands grab her and spin her around. With one hand gripping her hip and the palm of the other pressing against her back I repeat, "I said, bend over."

I guide her down until she's bent at the waist, her palms pressing into the mattress. I grab the condoms that I brought for no other reason than my need to always be prepared.

"You really are a boy scout, aren't you," she says with a laugh.

The urge to prove her wrong, show her just how bad this good boy can be increases by the second. With my cock wrapped and her pussy wet, I waste no time. My hands are on her hips, my fingers digging into her flesh. "Last chance to back out."

"Fuck me, Hunter."

I spread her legs a little further with my thigh, one hand releasing her hip and taking ahold of my dick to glide it over her entrance before I thrust fully into her in one motion.

Quinn Ford. Trouble with a capital T. Her sinner to my saint. My heaven to her hell. We crash together in a storm of fury. Endless pleasure surges through me. Her skin soft, her hair bouncing with each thrust into her, the way she rocks back against me, meeting me thrust for thrust. Perfection. Unison. Goddamn heaven sent.

No one has ever felt as amazing as Quinn does in this moment. No one has ever made me feel like Quinn does in this moment. I wrap my arm around her, my hand reaching for the swollen crux of her pleasure. Her head flies back, her hair flying as she cries out.

My free hand snakes up her body, wrapping around her throat. I give her a moment to decide if this is what she wants or not before applying enough pressure to make her gasp.

Every motion in sync as if we've worked tirelessly to master this. We barely know each other. Our needs, our wants, our likes and dislikes all foreign. Yet, in this moment somehow, I know how she needs it and which way she wants it. It feels so damn good to give it to her, to bring her pleasure, to see the look on her face when she turns to me. It's her eyes that do me in, the emotion I see in them.

I bury myself in her, grinding against her ass. Our connection deep, our bodies on edge, and all it takes to send me over is the soft mewl of my name falling from her lips. I come so damn hard that my body shakes, my head collapsing onto her back.

Neither of us move. Our bodies still joined, our breathing finally beginning to slow. Pants turning back into breaths, her voice still letting out these soft little sighs signifying she's coming down from her high.

I step back, sliding out of her and instantly missing the connection. When she faces me, her emotions are written all over her face. She stares at me, clearly unprepared for what just happened. Not the physical. We've done that before.

It's the emotions. The feelings I know she is having but doesn't understand. The vulnerability in her eyes intensifying with each moment that passes. She bolts to the bathroom and I don't stop her. I don't even try. I give her the space that she needs, while I clean up the wet mess we made and slide into a pair of shorts.

I'm kicked back on the bed, my back resting against the headboard. The last thing in the world that I want to do is scare her or make her feel cornered into sharing the bed with me. This is new to her, I get it. When she reemerges, stunned confusion written all over her face, I just smile at her.

She takes a seat next to me on the bed, her legs crossed at the ankles, just like mine.

"I'm sorry." The apology is unwarranted. In fact, I can't think of a single thing that she could even want to apologize for.

"There's nothing to be sorry about," I tell her. Hell, more than anything I should be thanking her because what just happened between us...wow. That was the shit dirty dreams are made of and everything I ever wanted.

"For running off. I just got overwhelmed."

"That makes two of us then," I say as I lean back, my hands behind my head.

She looks surprised. Like I couldn't possibly be taken aback by the intensity of everything that transpired.

"It's okay to be scared. Or nervous. Or whatever it is that you're feeling. And you don't have to explain anything to me. I hope you do, one day, but not now. Not until you're ready."

"Thank you."

I let out a yawn.

"We should get some sleep," she tells me.

"I can move back to the couch," I offer even though it's the last thing that I want to do.

"What? No. I don't want that." She turns in the bed to face me. "I'm sorry, I never meant for you to think that I didn't want this. Or us. I'm just scared."

"I was just trying to be a gentleman."

Her eyebrows raise. "You were far from a gentleman a few minutes ago."

"Would you have preferred if I were?" My eyebrows raise as well, challenging her to argue with me but also trying to gauge exactly what it is she likes.

"Not a chance," she smiles before pressing a kiss to my lips. She snuggles down into the covers then glances back at me.

"What?" I ask.

"Do you prefer to be the big spoon or the little spoon?"

I think of my dick pressed against her ass all night while we sleep. If we sleep. Because the thought of being pressed against her already has me ready to go again.

I slide under the covers, snuggle up against her.

"Really?" she says with a laugh.

"What can I say? When I find something that I like – I go with it."

My hand runs over her hip, down to her thigh moving it forward.

"Is this okay?" I ask.

Her head falls back against my shoulder as she sighs into the pillow. "It's more than okay."

***

I smile as I roll over, ready to pull Quinn into my arms and feel her body against mine again.

The woman I reach for is not there though.

In fact, she's nowhere to be found.

Chapter 23

Quinn

When I woke up in Hunter's arms two hours ago, my heart was racing and my mind spinning.

So many things were running through my head that I couldn't focus.

I needed air.

I needed space.

All because I realized that I need him.

I headed to the beach to enjoy the silence of the early morning. The only sound – the waves crashing against the sand. It's soft and serene and exactly what I need to help me deal with the shit storm in my head.

Last night was amazing. Everything about the entire day was. Sure, it was unexpected. Who would have ever thought that Hunter and I could be real? I barely had faith that we could pull off a fake relationship. How in the hell can I expect us to pull off a real one?

If my track record with men is any indication, we're going to crash and burn. And quick.

Especially if I tell him the truth. Or, rather, when. Even if it ends us, Hunter deserves to know what he's getting into. Who it is that he's getting involved with.

"Is this seat taken?" a deep voice asks from above me. The mere sound of it soothing my soul. Regardless of all the trepidation I have at the moment, my smile is automatic.

"I didn't run if that's what you're thinking," I say.

Hunter chuckles as he sits next to me. "Of course, you didn't. I'm sure you walked... right out the door." He throws my words regarding our first night together back in my face. It's not done with malicious intent, but rather with humor based on the smirk on his face.

"Aren't you going to ask why I'm out here?"

He shrugs. "Nope."

"Why not?"

"I told you last night, Quinn, I'll give you you're space, no questions asked."

"I owe you an explanation."

"You don't owe me anything," he says as he rests his hand over mine on the blanket.

Maybe I don't. I'm not entirely sure that's true. If I'm going to actually give this a go, try to be with him, I feel like he deserves to know. He should know who I really am. He should be able to see what he's getting into. To know not only if it's what he wants, but if it's worth it. If I'm worth it.

For so long I never thought I was. Never felt worthy of love or affection. Why would someone care about me when even my own parents didn't? Then I met Shane and he told me he loved me. And for the first time I felt the possibility. Until I found it was all a lie.

I think that was the hardest part to swallow. The fact that he lied because that lie is what had given me hope. It made me feel worthy of love for the first time of my life. And when it was ripped away by the truth...

"I left because I was scared. Terrified actually."

"Of what?" he asks. "If I..."

"No. No. Not you. You are perfect. It's me that isn't and I'm afraid that once you know me – you won't like what you see."

"I don't think that's possible, Quinn."

"How much has Mason told you about our childhood?"

He shrugs. "It's hard to say. I would say most of it, but... I always felt like there was something he wasn't telling me. I never wanted to push though. Everyone deserves to deal with their demons in their own way."

"Did you know that you were just supposed to be a means to an end? A plan we conjured up to befriend the rich kid at school, the one with the nicest clothes, getting dropped off in the fanciest cars? Mason was supposed to become your friend so he could steal food from you. It's wrong, I know, but..."

"You had to in order to survive," he replies. His voice is so filled with understanding that I'm the one who feels like they're on the outside looking in now.

"How can you not be angry about that?"

He has a soft smile then glances down at his hand. "Because I knew what was going on. Did you know he also stole money from my sock drawer?" He shakes his head and laughs. "Though I'm not sure if it's considered stealing if I kept putting it there for him. Same with the food."

"You knew?"

He shook his head. "I didn't know it was a plan, not for a long time. But I knew you guys were struggling. I knew he needed me. You both did. The truth is, I needed him too. I wouldn't be where I am today if it weren't for him pushing me. We may have both thought we were using each other but through that we became friends."

"I hated you for that, you know?" I make the admission, not something I had planned on telling him at this moment, but it feels right for him to know. "When you and Mason became friends, real friends, I resented you for taking away the only person that I had."

"I know you don't believe me, but I wanted to be your friend too, Quinn."

"I realize that now," I admit. My eyes have been unable to meet his throughout our entire conversation thus far. "I just always felt like you were looking down at me. That I wasn't good enough."

He tucks a strand of hair behind my ear. "I was looking, Quinn, that part is true. I was trying to figure you out. Trying to find a way to get you to trust me, to let me be there for you."

"There's something that I need to tell you, something you should know before we go any further. Things that I've done that could completely change the way you feel about me."

"I don't know what it is that you think would make me think less of you, but I assure you – nothing could be further from the truth. There is nothing that you could tell me would change what I feel for you."

"I wouldn't be so sure about that," I say, laughing through the tears that stream down my face.

"Try me."

The challenge in his words, my need to prove him wrong, all of it fuels the anger I speak with. "So, it doesn't bother you to know that I was more than willing to have sex with a man for money? Does that make you want me more? Is it a turn on?"

I shove off the blanket and walk closer toward the ocean. I need space from him, from my words, from everything.

"No, it's not a turn on, Quinn. It doesn't make me want to be with you more, but it sure as hell doesn't make me want to be with you any less. You did what you had to do to survive."

"That's just it. I didn't. I didn't go through with it," I tell him. "I couldn't just suck it up and do what needed to be done. Not how Mason always did. I backed out, I ran, I..."

Tears stream down my face. I turn away from Hunter, unable to face him as I give him the details. I can't bear to see the disappointment in his eyes when I tell him.

"The night I almost went through with it, I was home alone and one of my dad's friends, if you can call them that, stopped by. He made me an offer. Told me that for a night with me, he would make sure Mason and I were taken care of. Then he kissed me, and I remember thinking that it wasn't terrible... that I could do this. I could be the one to take care of us for a change." Hunter just stands there, not to close but not very far either, allowing me to ramble and get what I need to off my chest. He gives me the opportunity to show him the real me. The good, the bad, and everything in between. "I stood there, completely naked, the guy staring at me. He started... he started touching himself and...it made me sick. So sick and I couldn't. I couldn't go through with it."

His fingers caress the skin on my arms, an offer of comfort that I don't feel worthy of.

"I'm so sorry you had to go through that – all of it. No one should have to endure the things you two did."

When I turn to look at Hunter, I don't see judgment, or concern. Instead, there's emotion and kindness and for the life of me I can't figure out why it's there or why he would want to direct it at me.

"I don't want your pity."

"Good, because I don't pity you. Look at you, Quinn, look at the life you've made despite what you had to grow up with."

"The life I made?" She laughs. "Are you referring to the endless string of losers that I date? Or the fact that I got kicked out of college? Which of those points to this wonderful life you think I've made for myself?"

"How about the part where you have a roof over your head, always have, through nothing more than making it happen on your own because unlike me, you didn't always have someone to provide that for you? How about the fact that you got accepted into one of the best art schools in the country in the first place regardless of why you're not there anymore? Because one thing I am certain of, it's not for lack of talent. You showed me your work. You're amazing, Quinn. Everything about you amazes me."

I turn away from him, my arms hugging my body needing the comfort. "How is that possible?"

His arms wrap around me, comforting me when I had feared they would reject me. "Because it's you, Quinn. There has always been something about you. You're an amazing person and I hate that you don't see that." He pauses for a moment. "We all have pasts, our own struggles that we've had to endure. Nothing you've gone through or had to do makes me look at you any differently. All it does is make me want to be there for you to help you move past it. All I care about is us. Right here, right now."

"But..."

"But nothing, Quinn. Me knowing this, changes nothing."

"What if there's more? What if I've done things you can't forgive?" I ask thinking about Shane and how my actions weren't a far cry from what Layla did to him.

"There is nothing that you've done that I couldn't forgive."

"You say that..."

"I'm saying it because it's true. We all have pasts, Quinn. Despite what you think, I'm no saint. I've made my fair share of mistakes. All I care about is the here and now."

"You deserve better than me. Someone who can give you everything you want."

"All I want is you."

Every word he speaks, I want to believe it. I want to revel in it. "I'm afraid I'll disappoint you somehow. That you'll finally see the real me, the broken me, and you won't want me anymore."

"I see every broken piece, Quinn. And all it does is make want be there to help you put them back together. Because you can, Quinn. You can put those pieces back together."

"What about your family? Your career? The endorsements and charities? What if all of my dirty little secrets come out and somehow affect you?"

"It won't. But, if it does, then I'll deal with it."

"I can't risk doing anything to hurt you."

"Why don't you let me make that choice for myself, hmm? You told me your secret and I'm still standing here. I don't plan on, nor do I want to, go anywhere. Say you'll give us a chance. Make a real go of this fake relationship with me."

"A chance for what exactly, Hunter? We barely get along. We have nothing in common."

"And yet, here we are. Getting along. Enjoying each other. And I'm not just referring to the sex. All I want is a chance to show you... to prove to you that we can be good together."

"You do realize how absurd that sounds, right? Me and you together?"

"What can I say... you were right. You can be *very* convincing," he says with a wink.

I move toward him, and for the first time since we started talking, I look him in the eyes. "Are you sure about this Hunter? Like really sure?"

His hands cup my face. There's a twinkle in his eyes and a smile on his lips. "I have never been more sure of anything in my life."

Chapter 24

Quinn

"I told you so," Claire squeals into the phone. "How was it?"

After our chat on the beach, Hunter went in search of breakfast and I went in search of my phone so I could call Claire to get all of this excitement off my chest.

"I'm not answering that," I tell her.

No sooner do the words fall out of my mouth is she squealing again. She thinks she knows something. She thinks she's right. And she is.

"Oh God," she groans. "At least tell me this... was he nice or naughty? Because I picture him being nice and taking his time and..."

"And you would be wrong." Partially at least.

"You are getting me all riled up over here with no one to take care of it."

"I'm sure your vibrator will do just fine," I say with a laugh. "Just please don't picture him while you're doing it."

"Why? Are you guys like a couple now?" When I don't answer, her squealing resumes again.

"Will you stop doing that, please?" I laugh.

"You like him, you really, really like him."

"I wouldn't go that far," I lie as I desperately try to contain my excitement and not squeal in delight like she is.

"Ahh. You do. This is so amazing."

I plop down on the bed. "What's not to like? He's perfect. Exactly what every girl's dreams are made of."

"But?"

"Not a but so much as a... he's not what girls like me end up with."

I can practically see Claire roll her eyes at me. She hates when I say things like that. Her voice is loaded with frustration when she speaks. "I am so sick of you saying that. You're an amazing person, Quinn. You've overcome so much, and you have such a big heart. You just have to quit putting up these walls to keep people out. Let him in, let him see the real you. Not the girl who argues her way through relationships because she doesn't think she deserves anyone except assholes like Shane."

"He wasn't that bad," I say trying to defend myself. But who am I kidding?

"A yeast infection isn't that bad. He was awful," Claire replies. "Not only was he was married and screwing you. God only knows how many other students he's done it too."

Admittedly, the thought has crossed my mind. And grossed me out. He was the professor. He was seducing students. Yet, I'm the one that had to leave school. While he is still there probably doing the same thing to others that he did to me.

"Promise me one thing, Q."

"And that would be?"

"Don't push him away. Give it a real shot. You deserve that much."

The door to the hotel suite opens and Hunter stands in it with a bouquet of flowers in one hand and breakfast in the other. I shake my head, the smile on my lips automatic. "I don't think I could if I tried. I have to go; I'll see you in a few days."

"Details. I want details when you get back. Positions, size..." I disconnect the call that we were having on speaker phone.

"Hi," I say softly. I'm only slightly embarrassed by the fact that he caught me. And only because I know he's going to tease me about it.

We may have found a much better footing, but let's be honest some things aren't going to change. And I'm okay with that. I like that. I like us just the way we are. It's partially why taking this next step with him scares me. Because if we've finally found this common ground, what happens if the earth starts to quake and through no intentional fault of our own we come apart? How do we exist then?

"Should I be worried about what you told her?" he asks.

"I don't kiss and tell."

"That's too bad, it's always nice to get rave reviews."

"Is that what you think I would give you? Five stars?"

There's a shake of his head. "Seven out of five... minimum."

My gaze falls to the flowers he's still holding. "Are those for me?"

"These?" he asks, holding them up. "Nah, I got them for Mason. They're his favorite."

"You forget that I've seen you two together. I know that's a good possibility."

"I am pretty sure I proved last night where my desires lie." He hands me the bouquet. "If you need me to, I'm more than willing to prove it again and again. Whatever it takes. I'm willing to make the sacrifice for us."

"Sacrifice huh?"

"Definitely a worthy one."

I bring the bouquet to my nose and inhale the sweet scent. "They're beautiful."

"You're beautiful," he says as he presses his lips to my cheek.

Why he thinks a kiss like that is going to satisfy me, I have no idea. Not when he knew exactly what to do to satisfy my body. Unless of course he's trying to torture me. Which, after last night, I wouldn't put past him.

I set the bouquet on the bed and step up onto my tip toes. My lips begging for his. "Kiss me."

"I would but..."

"But?" I laugh. "Is the honeymoon already over?"

"Actually, it's just beginning. That's why I can't kiss you. Because if I do, I'll never stop. And I have other plans for you tonight."

"So much for you being fun," I tease. His hands rest at my waist and just the feel of our bodies together has every single nerve ending in my body quivering with anticipation. I crave his kiss, need his touch. As if it's not bad enough that we have to follow this itinerary, now he's going to torture me denying me a kiss?

"This better be good," I tell him.

"Oh, it is."

There isn't a doubt in my mind that whatever he has in store form me will be better than good. Amazing even.

When his lips press to my forehead in a sweet kiss, I swoon. Without having to really do anything at all he's infiltrating my mind and my heart.

***

After breakfast, Hunter excused himself to take care of something. He refused to say what, or how long it would take, he just... disappeared. He returned several hours later and informed me that I had thirty minutes to get ready for our date. That's it. No indication of what it is or where we're going.

"Do I look okay?" I ask, doing a little twirl in front of him.

"You look perfect. You always do." My cheeks flush, my temperature rising as I thank my lucky starts Layla is such a complete idiot. Because just as sure as I am that I don't deserve this man, I am equally as sure that Maddox doesn't hold a candle to what she's let go.

As we make our way to our destination, wherever that may be, I keep catching him looking at me. It's not overt, but I see it. His eyes drift toward me every couple of moments and he gets this smile on his face as if he can't believe this is real. It's immediately followed by a squeeze of his hand. I'm not sure if he realizes what he's doing or that he's being so obvious about it, but I don't call him out when normally I would. Instead, I take pride and enjoyment in the stolen glances and the way he looks at me. There's this little twinkle if excitement in his eyes and I almost feel like a prize he's won when really it should be the other way around.

I'm the lucky one. I'm the one who's gaining everything in this situation.

"Where are we going?" I ask.

We've been walking forever and I'm starting to think he has me going in circles. If I didn't know better, I would swear we passed that tree before.

"It's a surprise."

"Hunter..."

"You're going to love it, I promise," he says.

"How much longer until we get to this surprise?"

"It's right behind you."

What? How can that be? We just came from behind me. I turn to look and there, the cabana that we had just walked past, the one I didn't pay attention to because I was busy arguing with him, is lit with candles and flowers.

I gasp as the sight, my hand covering my mouth as it falls open in shock. "You did this for me?"

"I did," he says softly. "It's ours. All night. And, all day tomorrow. Just the two of us and the beach. How does that sound?"

"What about the itinerary? Hudson and Hayley will..."

"Hudson is already aware and Hayley... she'll just have to get over it." Hunter's hand caresses my cheek. "I just want to be alone with you."

No words have ever sounded better in my whole life. "It sounds like heaven."

Chapter 25

Hunter

A nother gorgeous morning. And the best part of it is, this time when I wake up, I'm not alone. The gorgeous woman from last night, she's still in my arms.

For two people who did not get along less than a week ago, we sure as hell have seem to overcome our issues. We spent the whole night talking and laughing. We set the heavy stuff to the side and just enjoyed each other's company.

We talked about music, movies, we even played a drinking games – which she won.

It was an amazing night. Then when we were ready to pass out, we headed back to our room and made love.

Now, in the light of day, I snuggle into her a little more my fingers dancing over her skin trying to rouse her.

"Are you serious?" she giggles in a sleep drunk voice. "It's only been two hours since the last time you woke me up for sex."

"Are you complaining?" I ask her has I run my fingers down the curve of her back.

"Can we at least get some food first? I'm starving. You're burning up all my energy."

"It's just morning wood this time, I swear," I chuckle. "We have breakfast reservations in ten."

Her body rolls to face mine, her breasts pressing against my chest and making me rethink our reservation and consider some room service instead. We only have a couple days left before we head back to reality. A reality that I hope looks much different than it did before we arrived in paradise.

Like now as I look at her across the breakfast table. She worries her bottom lip between her teeth as she looks over the menu. She's still the same woman that I've always known but we're different. We understand each other now, know each other. And we both like what we see. What we've always seen but were just too damn stubborn to acknowledge. At least I know that's what it was on my part. I had been so focused on how I thought things should be, how they should look, that I overlooked the fact that some of the best things in life are a little wild and even a little different.

Layla was my standard – my norm. But now, I feel like I'm seeing a whole different side of the things, discovering new pieces of me. Or, maybe not new, but buried?

"Quit staring," she says.

"Nope."

"You're an idiot," she laughs.

Then there's that. The arguments that we used to have now turned into a playful banter. And it makes me wonder if there was some sort of hidden desire there all this time. Then I wonder when in the hell I started sounding like such a chick.

"You're one to talk." I look up to see Layla standing there.

Christ, why won't the woman go away?

"What do you want now?" I ask, my tone filled with irritation that I hope to hell she hears.

"We need to talk," Layla asserts.

I look over at Quinn and smile. "I'm a little busy."

"Yes, I'm sure she keeps you busy, but I doubt satisfied."

Fucking hell this woman is really pulling out the daggers today. I sit back in my chair, my arms folded across my chest and a smirk plastered on my face. "Do I not look satisfied?"

"You cannot be serious with this. She has blue fucking hair," Layla shouts. The restaurant is filled with the breakfast crowd and at the high-pitched sound of her voice, all eyes are on us.

"They're streaks," Quinn argues.

"You're ridiculous," she shouts. "The idea of the two of you is just absurd."

"Lower your voice," I instruct her.

"Not until..."

I stand, grab Layla by the arm and lead her away. I won't let her cause a further scene. I sure as hell won't let her speak to Quinn like that.

"What the hell is your problem?" I ask Layla. My voice is quiet, but harsh.

"I'm not the one with a problem. You are. You are making a huge mistake with Quinn," she says.

"That's rich coming from you. The way I see it Layla, I made a mistake with you... not Quinn."

"Look at her," she says glancing to where Quinn is sitting. Where I should be sitting with her. I look at her sitting there looking confused, hurt, and uncomfortable. I watch as she fiddles with the napkin until the waitress brings her drink, which she downs immediately. I watch how I've affected her, how she knows she affects me. I watch her struggle with what this means. And I'm right there with her.

The only thing I seem to be missing is what it is Layla wants me to see. Because all I see is Quinn, beautiful, sexy, unique, and a perfect fit in my arms. I see a strong woman who hides her vulnerability behind a mask of anger because she thinks of it more as a weakness rather than realizing how much stronger it makes her. I see a woman that I've misjudged most of my life – a woman I want to get to know better.

"I'm looking, Layla. I've been looking for months and all I see is..."

"Blue hair? Slutty clothes? An attitude and a reputation that will chase away every team, every endorsement? Because when I look at her, that's what I see. Trouble, Hunter."

Quinn is definitely trouble. With a capital T. She's also the exact kind of trouble I find myself wanting to drown in.

"You don't know anything about her," I assert.

"No one else will either. All they will know is what they see. And they will all see the same thing I do – a cheap slut."

"Then you're blind. Besides, you forgot one important detail."

"What's that?"

"I don't give a damn what you think. I don't give a damn what anyone thinks. I am with Quinn. I want to be with Quinn. Nothing you do or say is going to change that."

"At least you're not disputing the fact that she's nothing more than a..."

"If I were you, I would stop right there. I gave you a pass once. I won't do it again."

"You're making a mistake."

At just the right moment, Maddox walks up. "Nope. I already did that. Now I'm fixing it." For the first time since everything happened, I size up the guy that has essentially turned into my replacement. The star baseball player who thinks that his shit doesn't stink. The kind of guy who thought it was okay to fuck some girl in another guy's bed. "Enjoy your trip."

"Hunter," she calls after me, but I ignore not only her words but the woman who is saying them.

I slide back into my seat at the table moments after our food arrives. "Looks like I'm just in time."

"Mm-hmm." Quinn's looking down at her plate, picking at the food.

"I'm sorry about that. Hopefully, she won't be bothering us anymore."

"At least it looks like our plan worked. She's jealous as hell."

"I never wanted to make her jealous."

"Isn't that the whole reason we started this thing in the first place?" Quinn asks before taking a bite of her pancakes.

I'm not really sure what I wanted to do, or why I thought having a date here with me would make it easier. But making Layla jealous wasn't even a thought. Why make a woman I no longer want, jealous? It's not as though I want to get back with her. I would be perfectly happy if I never had to see her again. That was the problem. That's what started all of this. The fact that I had to see her. With him.

"I guess more than anything I wanted a distraction. Something, someone to keep me from having to focus on Layla and her new boyfriend. But I don't care about that anymore. Because my distraction turned out to be a lot more than I bargained for."

"Did she now?" she asks leaning across the table.

"She did. She's exactly what I've been missing in my life."

"You shouldn't say things like that."

"Oh? Why is that?"

"Because she might start to believe you."

"Then I guess I better say them more."

Quinn and I lock eyes and the whole world slips away.

"I don't know if I can handle this." My head turns at the sound of Mason's voice. "You two getting along is creepy enough. Holding hands and staring at each other all dreamy like?" He sticks his finger down his throat making a gagging sound.

"You're an asshole, you know that?" I say with a shake of my head.

"So, what's on the agenda for today, kids?" Mason asks ignoring my question.

Quinn groans at the mention of the word agenda as she pulls out the sheet of paper with our itinerary on it. Just as quickly her frown turns into a smile. "A glass-bottom boat tour. That doesn't sound too bad, actually."

"Stuck on a boat with Layla for three hours? In what universe does that sound remotely good?" Mason chimes in. I have to admit, the man has a point.

The last thing I need is her saying or doing something to Quinn. Not after all the progress that we've made. I want Quinn to have time to adjust. To feel secure with the idea of us. I saw the flashes of concern in her eyes earlier when Layla approached. The hurt in them when Layla insulted her.

"We're not going," I remind her. "We're going to spend the day in the cabana."

"This actually looks really interesting," Quinn says. "Despite Layla."

I can almost see the wheels in her head spinning, the artist in her shining through.

"Then, we'll do it," I say.

"Are you sure?" she asks.

"Whatever my baby wants, my baby gets," I say. Mason cringes and makes faces.

As we head out of the restaurant Quinn is walking slightly ahead of us. "By the way, you'll be running interference today," I inform him.

"You think so," he chuckles.

"Quinn and I are uh, we're together. And the last thing I need is Layla doing something to fuck it up."

Mason nods, a smile on his face. "Thank fuck for that. Now I can quit worrying about her and these assholes and focus on..."

"Avery?" I supply the name of his other best friend. While I already know it's going to earn me a fresh slice of hell from him, I also know I'm right. He's just too blind to see it.

"You and Quinn need to get lives man. Avery and I are friends. Repeat after me. Ffff – friends."

I slap him on the shoulder. "Keep telling yourself that." Without continuing the argument that I know is bound to start, I jog to catch up to Quinn and pull her into my arms.

"Hunter," she squeals with excitement as her feet leave the ground.

Chapter 26

Quinn

The glass-bottom boat was even more beautiful than I expected. I'd never been on a boat, let alone one with a glass bottom where I could see every wondrous thing beneath us. Hunter studied me as I snapped photos with my phone of both of the ocean and of him. The latter of which he was not particularly fond of. He implored me to stop, eventually silencing me with searing kiss after searing kiss.

If he thinks punishments like that are going to get me to behave, he's sorely mistaken. If anything, it was nothing more than an invitation to behave even more badly.

Layla's eyes were on us the entire time. If our charade hadn't been working. It sure as hell is now. Not that any part of this is a charade anymore. It's one hundred percent real and I still can't believe it. Even more unbelievable than the idea of us being together is how easy it is. We fell into this comfort zone so quickly, so flawlessly. For him, maybe that's just how things are. Effortless. For me though, I've always struggled with people and relationships. Even with Claire. It takes me time.

I'm not sure if it's the familiarity that we have with each other having known each other a great deal of our lives or if it's just the way Hunter is, but there was no hesitation on my part like there usually is. Even after what Shane put me through, I find it easy to trust Hunter. To know that what he says is the truth.

Still, I wish I knew what Layla's game was. Something doesn't add up. Her cheating. Her staring. Her clear desire to be with Hunter. I can tell just by looking at her that she still loves him. So why? Why do this to him? To them? Did she simply make a mistake? It's not as though even the best of us are immune to doing it. Would he be willing to forgive her?

That, right there, is the biggest problem. My main problem. What if Hunter finds it in himself to forgive her? What if whatever this is between us just isn't enough?

Every fear runs through my head as I get ready for the nights event. Itinerary item number seven thousand thirty-two – Rush Nightclub.

At least it's more of an atmosphere that I'm prepared for. Short dresses, loud music, sexy moves. Much more my style than the more reserved feeling Hayley has imposed on the rest of this trip. That's not to say that all the activities are bad. The ATV rides, the glass-bottom boat. Those were both amazing. There were just some items, like the bingo game on the patio yesterday that just weren't quite my speed.

The look on Hunter's face when I step out of the bathroom is priceless. Without even trying to hide it, he takes me in. A low whistle escaping him when his eyes finally land on mine. "I'm speechless."

It's a nightclub, so I opted for one of the dresses that I already own. A sexy little blue number with the sides cut out at the waist so when Hunter's hands are on me, there is plenty of skin for him to burn.

"I'm not sure if I should cover you up or strip you down," he says as his tongue darts out to wet his lips.

"I could always do a strip tease for you. Maybe a little lap dance?"

It's my turn to admire him. The black dress pants that fit him like perfection, giving me and the whole world a view of his perfect taut ass. The gray button-down shirt with sleeves rolled up to his elbows looking like arm porn you never want to stop taking in. His blonde hair mussed, messy, and so sexy that I want to run my fingers through it leaving my mind to wander to how I did just that last night while his head was buried between my thighs.

"Do we have to go?" I whine as I sidle up to him. My fingers toy with the buttons of his shirt. "I'm sure I can find something much more entertaining for us to do."

"I don't doubt that, but..."

I bat my eyelashes at him. "Please, Hunter."

The crack of his neck, the groan he emits – I know I've got him. We're not going anywhere tonight.

At least we wouldn't be if it weren't for the incessant pounding on the door that Mason is doing. Followed by the shouting to open the door.

"Raincheck?" Hunter asks, as if I could say no to him.

Hunter opens the door allowing Mason and some red head to walk into the room. Hunter smiles at her and I feel a twinge of jealousy at the familiarity between the two even after the moment he and I just shared.

"It's good to see you, Ivy," he says as he pulls her in for a quick hug. I'm about to clear my throat to end their embrace when Hunter lets her go. "Ivy, this is my girlfriend, Quinn."

"It's so nice to meet you, Quinn," Ivy says a full, genuine smile on her face.

But I can't respond. I'm too awestruck by Hunter's words. Yes, I know we're together, but there is something about hearing him call me his girlfriend that just seems so surreal.

"You okay?" Hunter asks.

"Yes, I'm sorry. I just... your dress is stunning," I say to Ivy. And it is, the short cream dress with black and gold beading on it is just that – stunning. Just like the rest of her. "It's nice to meet you, Ivy."

"Shall we?" Hunter says as he moves back toward me, his hand on the small of my back.

I nod and the four of us head out the door.

"Are you sure you're okay?" he whispers the question into my ear as we wait for the elevator lobby.

"I'm perfect," I say leaning into him a little more. "You calling me your girlfriend, it just caught me off guard."

"Sorry. I don't have to. I didn't mean to make you uncomfortable."

"You didn't. I liked it. I guess I just still need to get used to the idea."

"You still want that? Don't you?"

The elevator dings and Mason and Ivy step inside. I look up at Hunter and take his hands in mine. My back is to the elevator.

"More than anything," I tell him. I step back toward the elevator tugging him with me.

We arrive at the club and are immediately escorted to a VIP area. The lounge is filled with liquor, food, and everything you could possibly want. All except a dance floor, sweaty horny people, and the energy of the club. I had always wondered what a VIP area would be like, what it would be like to be the person inside of it. Who they must be and how they must live. And now that I'm experiencing it firsthand, I'm not as impressed as I thought I would be.

"Not up to your... standards?" Layla asks when she approaches me.

"No, you're not."

"That's rich, coming from you of all people," she says.

I wish Hunter would get back with our drinks already. The sooner I down it, the sooner I can get him on the dance floor.

"Is there something I can do for you?" I ask trying to appear unaffected by her presence when in reality I am bubbling inside with rage.

There are dozens of people here for this wedding. Most of which I have never even spoken to or made eye contact with. This woman though, the one who cheated on her boyfriend and is here with her new one, you would think would be slinked away in a corner somewhere or at least trying to maintain her distance. Oh, no. Not Layla. She makes sure she is front at center at all times.

"I just wanted to let you know that I will figure out what it is that you're hiding. And when I do?"

Her pause after the question is overly dramatic for her.

"You'll what?" I ask with little emotion to my voice. My lack of concern over her threats infuriates her.

"I'll out you to Hunter." She stands there looking proud with her hands on her hips and a smug smile on her face.

"Unlike in your relationship with Hunter, he already knows all my secrets," I lie hoping to deter her from pursing her endeavor. If she were to find out about Shane and tell Hunter? There isn't a doubt in my mind he would hate me.

"We'll see about that." Layla tosses an evil smile my way before walking toward her new boyfriend.

The minute Hunter returns, I plead with him to dance with me. My fingers are gripping his shirt trying to get him to budge.

"What's the rush?" he asks. "Did something happen?"

"I just really want to dance," I assure him. "Please? If you dance with me. I promise I will take every inch of your cock into my mouth until it hits the back of my throat and let you..."

"Stop."

I smile against his ear. He didn't tell me stop because he thinks I'm being inappropriate or because this isn't the time or place. No, it's because of the hardened appendage I feel pressed against my stomach.

"Your damn mouth can make me come without even being on me," he whispers back to me. "Dance floor. Now."

Dancing does little to help his situation though. If anything, it only makes it worse. Harder to deal with.

Most of the group has made their way down to the dance floor. Even Mason and Ivy. We're all dancing all having a great time. Even Hayley has seemed to warm up to me. Maybe she can see the difference too. Maybe she finally sees Hunter and I as together.

"I'm going to get a drink," I shout.

"I'll come with you," Hunter says. There is an eager look in his eyes. As tempted as I am to take advantage of that, I'm having fun. For the first time in my life I feel like a part of the group, not the girl on the outside looking in.

I shake my head. "I'll be right back."

A chaste kiss and I'm on my way.

More than just a drink, I needed a moment to breathe, to take in the life that I'm living currently. It's so unlike anything I've known. I'm not talking about being in paradise, or the fancy resort we're staying at. I'm talking about Hunter. About happiness. Real true happiness for the first time in my life. As I take a sip of the drink in my hand, I look down at the club beneath me. Hunter is still on the dance floor, albeit much less animated than he had been before but he's trying.

Maybe he's right. Maybe I do deserve this. I sure as hell am enjoying it.

"All alone?" a masculine voice says from behind me.

When I turn to see who it's coming from, I'm surprised to find Maddox standing there. "I just needed a break," I tell him before turning my attention back to Hunter.

"Me too," he says. This time his voice is much closer, much deeper.

"I'll leave you to it." I try to skirt past him, but he blocks me. I sigh. "What? What do you want?"

"You," he says.

"Not happening."

I move again, but his hand presses against my stomach and presses me against the window. He gives me a wicked smile.

"You don't have to fight it. I saw the way you've been looking at me."

"You're delusional." Why in the hell would I bother looking at him when I have Hunter? I haven't taken my eyes, or my hands for that matter, off him all night.

Maddox's presence suddenly feels like a set-up. A way for Layla to get Hunter alone maybe? A way to make me look like a cheater in front of Hunter?

"Whatever it is that you think you're doing; it's not going to work."

"It already is," he says. I glance down at the dance floor and watch as Layla approaches Hunter. Before I can see anymore, Maddox grabs my chin and yanks my head toward him. "Now, where were we?"

Chapter 27

Hunter

Layla's standing in front of me. Quinn still hasn't returned. Something doesn't feel right. Something feels off.

"Where's Maddox?" I ask Layla.

"Don't worry. I'm sure he's being occupied," she smiles.

My hands grab her arms and pull her away from me. "Where the hell is he?"

Her eyes widen at the tone I take with her, the one that despite the raging music is clear as day. She still doesn't speak though. She just stares at me, stunned.

"Tell me," I shout.

"Up...upstairs," she stutters.

I release her before rushing back to the VIP room where I am certain Quinn is alone with Maddox. I'm also certain I'm going to find them in some kind of compromising position. All I can think is to rescue Quinn. Because whatever is going on, it's not by her choice. And she has had enough men in her life trying to make her do things she doesn't want to do.

When I walk into the room, the picture before me is exactly what I expected. Maddox's hands are on Quinn and there is a terrified look in her eyes. The sight infuriates me. It makes me see red and provokes me to do things I wouldn't normally do. Like unleash on this asshole.

"Get. Your. Hands. Off. Her." I say the words calmly. I'm giving him a chance. One chance.

When he doesn't do as instructed, I lose it. He laughs as I charge toward him. The wrecking ball that I am on the football field taking over the teddy bear that I usually am off it. "I said get your

Goddamn hands off her." This time I shout the words with an intensity that even startles me. My hands grab his shirt as I pull him off her and throw him to the floor. I drop to my knees, my fist cocked back ready to pummel him.

"Hunter, no," Quinn calls out. I focus on the desperation in her voice, the fear. Fear that he put there. Fear that her father's "friends" put there. I may not be able to teach those assholes a lesson, but I sure as hell can teach this one.

I feel my fist connect with Maddox's cheek. Then again. Then everything goes dark, blank until I feel hands on my arms pulling me back, Mason's voice backing them telling me to stop.

It isn't until he shouts "Enough!" that his voice truly breaks through though.

"He touched Quinn," I grit out between clenched teeth. There's a hiss of him sucking in air, air that escaped his lungs the moment why I was doing what I was doing registered. The overprotective brother taking hold.

"Let me handle him. You get Quinn out of here." Mason's instructions are clear. And as much as I want to continue unleashing a punishment on this douchebag, I want her away from all this even more.

That's when I hear it, her voice calming the storm that's raging in my head. "I'm okay, Hunter. Please. Just take me back to our room," she's pleading with me. The red I saw dissipating at the sound of her words.

I pull out of Mason's hold, my arms enveloping Quinn immediately. "You're sure you're okay?" I ask, my voice begging for the truth but hoping I don't hear what I fear.

"I'm okay. You got here before he could do anything," she assures me, and I hope to hell it isn't a lie to calm me. "Please Hunter, let's just go."

"You swear to me he didn't do anything?" I ask her as I shut the door to our room behind me.

The entire way back here we were both silent. Me trying to get my temper under control and her trying to wrap her head around what just happened, I'm sure. Or maybe not. Maybe she's pissed at me for interrupting or going all possessive caveman on her. I'm not really sure what to think. Especially now as I wait for her to answer.

She stands at the floor to ceiling windows, her arms wrapped around her staring at the ocean. I shove my hands in my pockets to help stamp down my need to touch her. I want to offer her comfort, but I also know that there's a good chance she may not want it. She may not want anything I have to offer.

"He didn't do anything." Her voice is soft and sad and I'm not quite sure if I believe her. She turns to me abruptly. "Layla wants you back. I don't know what game she's playing or why she slept with Maddox, but... she still loves you. She still wants you. If she didn't, she wouldn't go to these lengths."

"And?"

"And, if you want her if you still love her, I understand. I..."

Two strides. That's all it takes me to reach her. My hand framing her face, my eyes boring into hers desperate for her to see just how much emotion I hold for her. "I don't know why or how or when things between us changed and I sure as hell don't know how it all happened so fast, but..." I press my lips to hers, soft and gentle. "I know I have never been happier than I have been these past few days. I don't want Layla. I don't love Layla. All I want is you and to see wherever this goes."

"You're sure? Because I wouldn't be upset. I mean, I would, obviously, but..."

"Shut up," I laugh. "There is nothing to discuss. Nothing to question. You, Quinn Ford, are it for me. The only thing I wish is that I had seen it sooner."

"Then prove it," she tells me. Her hands grip my shirt, pulling it apart at the center. "Show me how much you want me. Show me how much I matter to you."

"Actions speak louder than words."

"They sure as hell do."

In an instant we crash together. Her hands working the belt at my waist, mine tugging the metal of her zipper down with haste. Clothes discarded, shoes stepped out of, hands becoming a frenzied mess. I pick her up, her legs wrapping around my waist and my dick begging to be inside her.

When her lips meet mine, her tongue sweeping into my mouth dancing with my own, promises of what it would be like if she were to slide it against my cock. Fucking hell. I press her up against the door, urgency in every move, every thrust. A sting slides down my back as her nails dig into my shoulders.

Pants, moans, and expletives fall from both of us. Needing to be deeper, needing to send her over the edge I sweep the items off the desk next to us before setting her there. She lies back, her hands gliding to her breasts, massaging them, as she waits patiently for me. I have no patience left. Not when it comes to her. There's only want and need, greed and hunger.

She cries out my name. The punishing motion I fuck her with only causing her to beg for more.

Between the sounds of passion, I hear what sounds like knocking on the door. The old Hunter, he would have stopped. He would have answered the door. He would have cared if people heard her cries and pleas. Not this Hunter. Not me. I'm more than willing to let the whole world know exactly what Quinn and I are together, how amazing we are. And there isn't a damn thing in this world that would stop me now. Not when I feel her tighten, not when I feel her orgasm ready to hit.

And when it does, when she screams my name, I fall over the edge with her.

"Someone's at the door," she says.

"Was at the door. Pretty sure they got the hint we're busy."

"That was anything but a hint," she laughs.

She's still sprawled out on the desk with me between her legs. I bend, pressing a kiss to her flat stomach. "Do you have any idea how amazing you are?"

"I aim to please."

Please? She surpasses pleasing me. I don't think there is even a word to describe how the woman makes me feel.

"Is someone crying?" Quinn asks lifting her head off the desk. I hear it too.

The door. What if it was an emergency? Shit.

I grab a towel from the bathroom and wrap it around my waist. I pull the door open to find Layla standing there. Tears streak her face, her nose fire red from crying.

While it serves her right considering what I had to walk into a part of me still feels bad. "Layla." I say her name softly, an apology of sorts.

"You're really with her, aren't you?"

"Yeah, I am."

She swipes at the tears. "You can do better. You deserve better."

I'm about to argue with her, tell her that she doesn't know what she's talking about. Tell her that she doesn't know or understand Quinn or what we have together. Then it dawns on me that I don't have to tell her shit. I don't have to explain myself or my relationship. She lost that right the minute she let Maddox slip into her.

"And I finally found it," I reply before shutting the door.

When I turn back and look at Quinn, she's smiling. "That is the sweetest thing anyone has ever said about me."

"Oh, you thought I meant you? Sorry. I was talking about my new shoes."

"You do your shoes the way you just did me?" Our eyes drift down to the shoes next to the door. "The fact that I can actually picture that..."

"Don't even."

Laughter fills the room.

Laughter. Sex. Happiness.

Quinn.

Trouble with a capital T.

The exact kind of trouble that I may very well be falling in love with.

Chapter 28

Hunter

After the events that transpired last night, Quinn and I steered clear of everyone from the wedding. We hid in our room, ordered room service, and then snuck off property to enjoy some of the local shopping and scenery.

As amazing as our day was, there was one thing we couldn't skip. The rehearsal.

"I wouldn't be upset if you didn't come," I assure her. After what Layla did, I wouldn't blame Quinn for wanting to leave altogether.

"It's fine. I'm fine." She squeezes my arm as we walk. "Besides, I have a big handsome football player who isn't going to take his eyes off me, let alone his hands."

"Damn right, I won't."

If Maddox so much as looks in her direction, I have every intention of finishing what I started last night.

Actions speak louder than words and I would sure as hell hope that even Maddox would understand that my fist in his face means to stay the fuck away from Quinn. I don't put much past the guy. Or Layla for that matter.

Having been together since our senior year, I really thought I knew everything about Layla. Now, I don't feel like I ever really did. Who is this woman? Why is she hell bent on trying to hurt me?

"Hunter, I mean it. I am fine. Please don't do anything crazy."

Depends on what your definition is. Because defending my girlfriend? Prying some assholes hands off her? None of that sounds crazy to me.

"As long as he stays away from you."

It's the best I can give her. I'm not making promises that I can't keep. And promising to stay away from Maddox when the guy seems to want to claim everything that's mine, is a promise I can't be sure to follow through with.

First stop is the gazebo where the ceremony will be performed. As the priest provides direction and instruction, I find myself unable to take my focus off Quinn. How hard can it be to walk down an aisle anyway?

Even though Maddox doesn't seem to be anywhere in sight and Quinn is seated with my parents, protected, it's not enough. She's my girl, my responsibility and I'll be damned if anyone goes near her again.

I feel an elbow to my ribs. I'm standing next to Hudson and apparently got caught not paying attention if the scowl on Hayley's face is any indication. "Sorry."

The rehearsal continues, each step of the process outlined in detail. I shouldn't be surprised considering this is Hayley we are talking about.

After an hour of unneeded instruction, the rehearsal finally ends. Just as I'm about to step away from my best man duties I feel a hand on my arm. Instinctively my mind automatically jumps to it being Layla and I begin to tug my arm away. But, when I look, it's Hayley standing there.

"Sorry, Hayls," I say in apology of my lack of participation in the rehearsal.

"Don't apologize," she tells me as she loops her arm through mine. We begin to walk slowly. "In fact, I should be the one apologizing. I shouldn't have let Layla come. I should have..." She shakes her head. "I'm sorry, Hunter. I know this trip has had to be difficult on you."

"I thought it would be," I answer honestly. "But, Quinn, she made it much more enjoyable than I ever could have imagined."

"You really like her, don't you?"

"I do."

"I told Layla that I didn't want to see Maddox tonight. That if she chose to bring him to the wedding tomorrow, I wouldn't stop her, but that they both needed to stay away from you and Quinn, or I would have no hesitation having them removed."

"No worries. I have no intention of taking my eyes off Quinn. Though, I do promise to focus better tomorrow for the actual festivities."

Hayley presses a kiss to my cheek. "I appreciate that." She begins to walk toward Hudson but stops and turns back to me. "Oh, and, for what it's worth, I agree with Hud. I think Quinn is good for you."

"Me too," I agree.

"Stare much?" a voice asks from behind me. My smile is instantaneous, and I can't help but pull her in for a kiss when I turn to her.

"It's your fault."

"Mine? How's that?" she laughs.

"You're the one sitting over there looking beautiful. How am I supposed to look at anything else?"

"You flatter me, Adams." We lace our fingers together. As we do, as we stand here gazing at each other smiles on our faces, neither of us have a care in the damn world. Hell, I'm not sure if we even realize there is a world outside of us. Quinn breaks the spell, "Come on, let's get this dinner over with because I'm starving."

"Wait. Wouldn't you want to..."

She raises an eyebrow, the corner of her mouth twisted up slightly. She's starving, but it's not for food. I return her sexy grin with one of my own.

"No worries about that, sweetheart. We don't have to wait until after dinner."

"What do you mean?" she asks as I begin to lead us away. "Hunter. What are you... where are we going?"

"Detour." It's all I say. It's all she needs to know.

If she's starving. I'm downright famished. She is a hunger I intend to satisfy. Immediately.

I push on the door to my right. Locked. To my left. That's locked to. Another door and bingo. It opens with force, striking the wall behind it. I pull her against me and kiss her. I lock the door behind us. The room is dark, nothing more than a dim light shining through a vent.

"Hunter," she exclaims, thrill and excitement in her voice. "What are you doing?"

My lips making my way down her neck. "Do you really have to ask?"

"Here? Now?"

"You're starving. I'm famished and you are the only damn thing that will satisfy me. Got a problem with that?"

Through the strands of light, I can see the smile on her lips, the intrigue in her eyes. She doesn't think I have it in me. Obviously, she doesn't realize how desperate she makes me. I turn her until her back is against my front. My hands gliding across her body, underneath the fabric of the short dress she's wearing. Fingers grip the material, bunching it in my hands and tugging it up until what I want is before me, wet and waiting.

"Do you want me, Quinn?" I ask, my voice husky and dripping with desire. I have never wanted anything in my life like I do this woman.

"Yes," she says her voice nothing more than a whimper.

My fingers slide between her parted thighs. I had hoped she was ready for me but feeling her slickness is more than gratifying. With her legs parted, her fingers gripping the shelf before us, and the sexy little smirk she tosses at me when she looks back in my direction, I'm done. With a haste like I have never experienced before, I undo the button and zipper on my pants and let them fall to the floor. My arm snakes around her waist, forcing her body to become flush with mine.

"Christ, all I want is you."

"I'm yours. Every piece of me is yours, Hunter."

I stroke my cock in my hand as her words settle over me. "Every piece?"

She knows exactly what I'm referring to. The most important piece, the piece that I know she doesn't allow anyone near willingly or without strict consideration.

Her hand takes a hold of me, replacing my own. "Yes, Hunter. Even my heart."

My head drops to her shoulder, my lips feathering kisses on her suntanned skin. I don't know how it happened, I sure as hell don't understand how it happened so quickly, but fuck if it isn't everything. "I love you, Quinn," I whisper as I push into her. Our cards are on the table, our feelings on our sleeves. Me, buried inside of her feels fucking amazing and just intensifies what I already know.

Quinn Ford infiltrated my mind, my body, and now my Goddamn soul.

She cries out and tempted as I am to quiet her, I let the sound fill the room. Her moans as I fill her, her whimpers as I pull back, as if she fears I am walking away. Christ, I could never do that. Not from sex, not from her. Not willingly at least.

Everything about this woman invades my mind and my body gives to her exactly what it wants, what she needs.

We move together, not hurried, but not exactly gentle either. We don't have much time, but I fully intend on taking advantage of what little we do have. My hand moves from its spot on her stomach down between her thighs again, my thumb strumming over her clit.

She softly says the words more, *faster*, *harder*. Quiet or not, each is said with force, instruction, determination. I do as she says, my sole goal to please her, to make sure that this woman that more than satisfies every part of my being is exactly that – satisfied.

She screams out my name as she tightens around me. Tumbling over the edge, she pulls me with her until we've both hit our high and landed in an orgasmic bliss.

"You're full of surprises," she says.

"You haven't seen anything yet," I tell her.

"Oh?"

I give her a wink. "We still have a flight home."

Chapter 29

Quinn

When Hayley first extended the invitation to me to join her and her bridesmaids in the spa the morning of the wedding I wanted to decline, to scream hell to the no. With the ruse that Hunter and I were putting on, I couldn't do that so instead I accepted, begrudgingly. The idea of spending a day in the vicinity of a bunch of women who hate me made me sick to my stomach. Hell, even a root canal sounded more appealing.

Things were different now, though. Hunter and I, we aren't a ruse anymore. We're real. One hundred percent real. The thought alone brings a smile to my face. While I haven't had too much interaction with the other ladies, most have been pleasant and kind. Even Hayley and I had a great time dancing the other night and then again sipping cocktails under the moonlight with Hunter and Mason. I may have judged her and her friends too harshly. The same way I had judged Hunter. I realize now that I have spent way too much time disliking people for being better off than me rather than getting to know them.

The only thing left to dread now: Layla.

Between the debacle that her and Maddox created, the fight that ensued, not to mention her showing up at our doorstep all teary eyed, I can't help but dread whatever fresh hell she has conjured up for me today.

When I step into the spa, the rest of the ladies are already there. Hunter has a funny habit of not wanting to let me go and then explaining with great length exactly how much. Everyone is sipping cucumber water and relaxing in their robes and slippers with both their hair and make-up the picture of perfection. Me on the other hand, my hair is in a knot atop my head and my skin is completely bare.

"You made it," Hayley exclaims. She comes over to me and pulls me in for a hug.

It's a far cry from the disapproving look she gave me when I first arrived with Hunter. I revel at how much has changed in the course of the week. Including me. I feel free for the first time ever. I feel so light and carefree as though I could just float away. All thanks to Hunter. A man who was nothing like I imagined he would be. And believe me, Mason has made me apologize to him profusely for all the shit I've given him over the years about his friendship with Hunter.

"I did," I say as she pulls me in for a hug. "Sorry I'm a bit late."

"Let me guess, Hunter?" She flashes me a knowing smile. "Must run in the family."

Layla's face contorts into a look of disgust and it only serves to egg me on and make me want to give gory details. Details that I would have to make up because no way in hell am I giving them the truth. Like how the nice guy somehow manages to become the epitome of a bad boy when it comes to sex. Or how he owns my body with every touch, every kiss. Definitely not the sound of his voice when he commands me to bend, to move, to anything because that sound alone damn near makes me orgasm. And I sure as hell am not going to give details like how well-endowed he is. Like holy shit, is that thing real?

"Then you are one lucky woman," I say. "Because... damn. I'm not going to be able to walk straight by the time we get home. I mean, without school and stuff getting in the way, literally all we do is...."

"No one cares," Layla chimes in.

"I bet between the two of you we could get some good Hunter stories," one of the other bridesmaids says. "You know, just in case he's ever available again."

"He will be, soon, I'm sure." Layla smirks at me.

"I wouldn't be so sure about that," I tell her returning her smirk.

"Okay, girls, let's not do this. Okay?" Hayley says.

As much as I would love to taunt Layla right now, really stick it to her, I won't be rude to Hayley. She is Hunter's family, and despite a rough beginning she's been kind to me.

Rather than engage Layla any further I ask, "What's first?"

The spa director enters the room and begins to go over our plans for the day. Thankfully, the things she describes, we don't all have to participate in together. The less time I can spend with Layla, the better. The woman has a way of getting under my skin and today is Hayley's day. I have no intention of causing any problems or creating any drama. I just want to do my best to relax and enjoy the day. So, when the director hands me the clipboard to sign up for my spa treatments, I make sure that there isn't a moment where I would be anywhere near Layla.

Not that it means anything to her.

"Is this seat taken?" Layla asks plopping down in the chair next to me. "Oh goody." She slips her feet into the warm water. "I swapped with someone so you and I could have some time together to... get to know each other."

I sigh. Everything had been going so well, too. In fact, I found myself actually relaxing and enjoying my time, thinking about Hunter, and us, and what a future for us might look like. While it might seem like I'm jumping the gun, everything just feels so right. It's as though there has been some underlying attraction or emotion there that neither of us understood. And now that we do... I sigh again. This time it's a peaceful sigh. One that knows just how amazing Hunter and I are together.

I close my eyes trying to ignore her presence and return to my happy state.

"So... you and Hunter."

Breathe Quinn, I tell myself. The last thing I need to do is open my mouth and make matters worse.

"It's not going to last you know. He deserves someone better."

Funny, there is one thing that we actually agree on. "You're right, he does. Better than both of us," I say.

"I made a mistake. You are the mistake."

"Funny, he says that differently." Don't engage, I remind myself.

"Don't think that I'm not onto you," she says. "I know your hiding something."

"Am I interrupting?" a woman asks as she settles into the chair on the other side of me. I smile when I see Ivy's smiling face.

"I sure hope so," I reply.

She claps her hands together. "Oh goody. By the way, you and Hunter make the cutest couple."

Before I can speak Layla replies, "Not for long they won't."

"I had a great time with you guys the other night. And Mason, too, of course," Ivy replies completely ignoring Layla and her insane ramblings.

"Do I need to apologize for him?" I joke. Though with Mason, you never know.

"No apologies at all. He is such a sweetie. And, uh, who's Avery?" Ivy asks.

"A friend," I tell her. Though if he is talking about her while we're in paradise and he is surrounded by beautiful women, then all signs point to me being right. There is something more there.

Eventually Layla tires of listening to Ivy and I chat. She stands from her seat; her hands are on her hips and her desire to have the last word more than evident. "I will find out what it is you're hiding, and I will make sure that Hunter knows exactly who he's "dating"," she says. Refusing to dignify her threat with a response, I allow her to have the last word. And when she is finally gone from the room, leaves the room my body actually relaxes in my seat.

I hadn't realized how tense I had become with her sitting next to me. Even now, with her threat hanging over my head, I can't fully relax. For the moment, she knows nothing. Just a suspicion that I'm hiding something, which in fact I am. And if Hunter finds out what I'm hiding, there isn't a doubt in my mind that would be the end of us. While that is probably for the best, I'm not ready to let go yet. I'm not ready for my first glimpse at real happiness to disappear right before my eyes.

"You okay?" Ivy asks.

I plaster a fake smile on my face hoping she doesn't notice that it's not genuine. "I'm fine. She just... I can't stand her."

"No one can. I think the only reason she's even here is because her and Hayley grew up together. More out of obligation than anything," Ivy tells me. "I wouldn't worry about her. Now that Hunter smartened up, I'm sure she's just scrambling."

"I'm not so much worried about her as I am sick of her," I lie. Because I am a hell of a lot more worried about what she might uncover and what she would do with that information.

There's nothing in my record on why I transferred schools, I just... transferred. Unless you look at the records from Columbia. The grades, the professors, the note in my file on why it was suggested that I leave the school and find somewhere else to attend. Add in the rumors that ran amuck around campus and she would piece together quite a story. But that information, none of that would be easy to come by. Right?

Chapter 30

Hunter

Quinn stands in the doorway to our room looking like she's ready to fight.

"Uh-oh, am I in trouble?" I ask.

"So. Much. Trouble."

"Can I ask what I'm being charged with?"

A smile breaks through. "Rescuing me without me asking. Assuming that I needed saving when I didn't. How do you plead?"

"Guilty. So guilty. And I am ready to take my punishment. Whatever you want to do to me, I'm ready."

She raises an eyebrow at me. "You sure about that?"

"Oh yeah."

"Thank you. I didn't need it, but Ivy did make the day less dreadful."

"Everyone needs an ally sometimes. And since I couldn't be there for you..." I shrug.

Quinn walks further into the room, straight to the bed that I'm sitting on and straddles me. My erection is almost instantaneous. "You are making things very hard, Ms. Ford."

"I see that. Or I guess, I feel it?" She looks past me to the clock. "But if we don't hurry, we're going to be late. And you cannot be late, Mister Best Man."

"I suppose not. But there should be plenty of time between the ceremony and the reception to find a quiet closet somewhere."

"Oh no," she says. "You are just going to have to behave today. This is about Hudson and Hayley and..."

"Trust me, Hudson would be in complete agreement with my suggestion. In fact, we might have to fight him for that closet."

She shoves off me. "That's what I've heard. Seems both of you are incorrigible." Finally, she notices the garment bag hanging on the bathroom door. "What's this?"

"A little surprise," I say grinning broadly. "Open it."

She pulls the zipper down and opens the bag. Her hand comes to her mouth. "Hunter."

"Do you like it?"

"Like it? It's... it's.... you didn't have to do this."

Her hand runs over the soft blue fabric. The shade matching the streaks her in hair perfectly. Streaks that she thought I would want her to change when all I want is to embrace her just the way she is. I hope this gesture goes a small way in proving that.

"I saw it and the color blue reminded me of your hair." She hangs her head but lets out a small chuckle. "And I thought you would look amazing in it. Put it on."

"Words I never thought I would hear you say."

"Believe me, words I never thought I would say when it came to you."

She slides the jean shorts she's wearing down her thighs before tugging the camisole over her head. How I'm supposed to wait until tonight, I don't know. And the moment she slips into the dress, it actually becomes harder to resist her. Who knew more could actually be so damn sexy?

My eyes are glued to her as she twirls around. "So?"

"You. Look. Breathtaking."

"Thank you, so much for this." She runs her hands down her body in admiration of the dress causing me to groan. Looking at Quinn is enough of a turn on. Watching her touch herself, even if she is dressed is fucking lethal.

"It's my pleasure, really," I say watching her in it. Knowing that I'm going to be holding her in that dress as we dance the night away. And then, tonight as I take it off of her. I reach for the tux hanging next to where the dress had been. "Let's get this over with. The sooner I get you out of that dress, the happier we both will be."

I move to head to the bathroom. "Uh-uh," she says. She sits in the chair near the window and seductively crosses her legs. "My turn." I look at her confused, unsure what exactly it's her turn for. "Strip, Hunter."

Her tongue sweeps across her bottom lip before she pulls it in and takes it between her teeth. If Quinn wants a show, I'll give her a show.

My hands grip the material at the bottom of my shirt, slowly pulling it up, inch by inch. My eyes are locked on her, taking in every breath, every shift of her body in her seat, and every emotion that flickers in her eyes.

"Are you trying to torture me here?" she says.

"Payback."

When I finally pull my t-shirt over my head, I toss it at her. She catches it, bringing the material up to her nose and inhaling my scent. My hands move to my board shorts, the ones I've been wearing since Hudson, Mason, and I decided to try surfing this morning. A last minute guy's thing since all the women were occupied. When I slide them down revealing nothing underneath, Quinn smiles.

"That's what I'm talking about," she says. "You know, at the spa today, I was getting grilled about what it was like to be with the one and only Hunter Adams."

Completely naked, dick standing at attention, I stand before her. "And what did you tell them?"

"Not much. I didn't want you to get attacked by women, so I kept it simple. Said that I could barely walk straight after all of our extracurricular activities."

"Barely huh?" I laugh. "Going to have to make sure I turn that into a full I can't walk at all tonight."

"Bring it on."

God, how I want to do just that.

But the clock is ticking and if I don't get to the beach soon, Hudson is going to have my head. He might be a pain in the ass, but he's no fool. Keeping Hayley happy is top priority. And now, I understand that concept more than ever.

"Clothes. You need clothes," Quinn says as she gets out of the chair and walks over to my suitcase. "Here." She hands me a pair of boxers, her eyes drifting down my body. "Put them on. Now."

"And you say I'm the insatiable one."

"You have a problem with how much I want you?" she says as she turns away again.

"Not at all. Quite the opposite actually."

When I'm fully dressed Quinn faces me. "Yep, still not helping."

My hands drop to her waist and pull her against me. "The clothes don't matter. It's what's in here that makes all the difference," I say as I press my hand to where her heart is.

"You and your swoony lines. Let's go before my panties melt into a puddle on the floor."

"You first. I want to take in the view."

With an exaggerated sashay of her hips, Quinn walks to the door. "Coming?"

I think of the beach, her naked body standing before me asking that same question. The automatic response in my head, and my dick, still the same – damn close to doing just that.

Chapter 31

Quinn

"Absolutely not," I laugh.

Still, here he is, hands on me tugging at my waist, my hands, anywhere he can touch pleading with me to sneak off with him.

"Your whole family has eyes on us considering the bride and groom have gone missing. We are not doing this," I giggle.

The way he looks, eyes filled with desire and a bit of sadness at my rejection. The puppy dog look if you will. While I can't typically resist him, nor do I want to, this isn't happening. Not today. Not when all eyes are on us.

Or at least were until the bride and groom return looking completely disheveled.

"Let's do this," Hudson shouts.

"Pretty sure you already did," someone shouts back.

I stifle my laughter as I see the flush to Hayley's cheeks. But the rest of the crowd doesn't seem to have the same couth that I do. "That could be us right now. No way."

"I don't know," Hunter says. "Hudson looks pretty pleased. Pretty sure I would, too."

I slap his arm. "You would look more than just look pleased."

Hunter's mother is flagging him over. Now that the bride and groom decided to show, it's time to get the show on the road. Step one – the receiving line. "Go. You're needed," I say, giving him a slight shove.

His playful attitude changes and he stops dead in his tracks. I look in the direction where his gaze has fallen. Maddox. "Go. I'll be fine. He isn't going to try anything in front of all these people.

Besides... they saw their plan failed. I'm sure they'll come up with something new next time."

The moment I say the words, dread falls over me. Because while I don't have any knowledge of the what or the how of it, I am certain there will be a next time. Layla, for whatever reason, will always try to interfere.

"Stay where I can see you," Hunter tells me. I raise my eyebrows in response. "Please?"

I press a kiss to his lips before instructing him to go fulfill his best man duties. I take a seat on a nearby couch, far enough away, but still within his eyesight.

Mason takes a seat next to me. "So, this is really a thing huh? I'm going to have to get used to this."

"You always said I should give him a chance," I say with a shrug. "It's kind of your fault."

"Not exactly what I had in mind, but... you look happy."

Happy. It's exactly what I am and such a foreign concept to me. Struggling as we were children, a rash of bad boyfriends, followed by one experience where I thought I may have found my happiness only for it to implode and come crashing down on me.

"I'm scared," I admit.

"That's normal," Mason says. Not that he and his bachelor for life ways would know.

"What if it doesn't work out? What if I screw this up somehow? What if..." What if he finds out about Shane and ends up hating me?

"That's a lot of 'what ifs', Sis."

If only he knew the half of it. "I guess I'm just afraid that it's going to come crashing down on me."

"Pretty sure everyone's afraid of that. And you have more reason to than most. But, Q, Hunt's a good guy. He's going to do everything in his power to make you happy, to be there for you. You just have to let him."

"Easier said than done," I tell him.

As I watch him though, I realize, I already have. In more ways than I have ever let anyone before. Shane knew nothing of my past. All I told him was that my parents weren't in the picture. He never asked for an explanation, so I never gave him one. Hunter didn't have to ask. He already had an idea. Maybe that's what made it easier for me to open up to him. Or maybe it was just the kindness in his eyes.

If anyone would have asked me two weeks ago, hell, ten days ago, if I thought there was a chance in hell that Hunter and I would end up here, I would have laughed in their face and my answer would have been a resounding no. All because I never gave him a chance. Because I judged him rather than got to know him.

If they asked me now if I could ever see my life without him. The answer would be the same. No.

"Dance with me?" Hunter asks as he comes up from behind him. His lips are near my ear, his hands resting on my hips.

"I thought you'd never ask," I reply as I rest my head back against his shoulder.

"Really? I kind of thought I was a sure thing."

"For some things, yes," I tease.

He leads me to the dance floor. With finesse, he twirls me around before pulling me to him. We sway to the music, his arms holding me tightly. The fact that today is our last day in paradise, that tomorrow we head home to reality – to our real lives - is more than weighing down on me. Fear that once we aren't here, away from everything that life really has to throw at us, that maybe, just maybe we won't work.

Sensing the tension in my body, Hunter asks, "Penny for your thoughts?"

I rest my head against his chest, "Just thinking about tomorrow."

"Sudden fear of flying?" he asks. The tone in his voice leads me to believe that there is more to his words than what they are actually saying.

"Sudden fear of crashing is more like it."

"The plane? Or us?" He asks even though he already knows the answer. He rests his lips against the top of my head as he speaks. "It's not going to happen."

"How can you be so sure?"

As much as I want Hunter, I still can't be certain. Not in the unwavering sense that he is.

"Because I won't let it. I care about you too much, Quinn, to let anything get between us. You trust me, don't you?"

"Of course, I do." More than anyone or anything.

"Then believe me when I say that we are going to be fine. In fact, we might even be better than we are now."

I pull back at look up at him. "How is that possible?"

His smile meets his eyes, and it's filled with love. "Because we're only just beginning."

Our lips meet as the song ends and we are left standing in the center of the floor, the beat of the music turning to something with a quicker pace.

"I'm going to head to the restroom, I'll be right back," I say.

"I'll get us some drinks and think of an excuse to leave early."

I step out of the bathroom stall and head to the sink. I touch up my make-up and smile when I see the glow on my skin. It's not from the make-up or even the sun. It's happiness. It's Hunter. It's the crazy amazing effect he has on me. When I step back to leave, Layla enters.

"What now?" I groan as she does her best to corner me in the bathroom by blocking the door, removing any chance I have for escape.

Unless, of course, I fight her. Which I would love to do but I'm fairly sure that Hunter would frown upon it. And nothing, especially not Layla, is worth ruining what I have with Hunter.

"I finally figured it out. I thought I wouldn't, but I did."

"This again?" I laugh. "You're pathetic." As I head toward the door, Layla steps to the side. That was easy. Too easy. Something isn't right. No sooner does my hand grab the handle do I know just how true that is.

"I know about Shane." My head whips in her direction. "Or is it Professor Shane? Or Professor Powell?" She cackles like a damn witch as she spills the truth that I swore she couldn't have possibly known. "Did you moan out "Oh Professor" when you fucked him?"

"You don't..."

"Oh, but I do."

I let the door shut.

"I know that he's married. I know that you seduced him. I. Know. Everything."

She knows everything and nothing at the same time. The story she has, inaccurate, but there is still truth behind it. The truth that I had an affair with my very married professor. It doesn't matter how it happened, or who did what. It just matters that it happened. And there isn't a doubt in my mind that she's biding her time, dying to tell Hunter. There's an ache in my chest. That fear of crashing becoming more of a reality than I ever thought possible. There's a reason she's doing this. Something that she wants. Whatever it is, it's the same damn reason she tried to trip me up by throwing Maddox at me. It didn't work then, but she's not leaving me a whole lot of choice here. If Hunter finds out the truth, we're as good as over anyway.

"What do you want?" I ask. This little encounter is so much more than just two girls sharing secrets in the bathroom. No, this is blackmail, pure and simple. I have a feeling that I know what she wants and I'm already dreading having to do it.

"You and I both know that you don't deserve, Hunter. And this little secret you've been keeping..." she shakes her head and does a little tsk tsk, "it could destroy him." I'm about to protest, to argue how and why my life will in no way impact his – not the way she did. She holds up her hand to stop me before she speaks again. "Think what you want about me, Quinn, but I am looking out for Hunter. For his best interest."

"And you're in his best interest, right?"

A slight shrug of her shoulders. "Maybe, maybe not. But you? You most definitely are not. Do you have any idea what your little scandal could do to his reputation? To his endorsements? His charity? Not to mention that since you've walked into the picture the man has been involved in two bar fights? What next? What do you think it's going to look like when he's seen with a homewrecking party girl?"

"And let me guess, you would have no problem letting all of that just slip out?"

Her hand flies to her chest. Every motion exaggerated. "I would never."

"Just say what you have to say so we can get this over with." My patience for her threats is wearing thin. I just want to hear her say it. I want to know what I'm dealing with so I can figure out how the hell I am going to break Hunter's heart when it's the last thing that I want to do.

"Here's the deal. You end whatever this thing with you and Hunter is, and I will keep my mouth shut."

"He won't buy it," I protest. Not because I'm trying to get out of this, but because it's true. There is no way Hunter will buy that I don't want to be with him. Not without trying to talk me out of it. Not after what we've shared. "And he sure as hell won't give up that easy."

"Figure it out."

"Fine," I reply agreeing to her terms.

"Fine?" she repeats as though she can't believe I'm giving in this easily.

I can't believe I am either. But she's right. One of the best things about Hunter is his pristine reputation. It makes him an even hotter commodity than he already is. He would make any team look good on top of him playing his ass off for them. And scandal, even something he isn't directly involved with could hurt that and any sponsorships he would receive. Not to mention the charity work I know he was hoping that his career would help with.

"Yes, fine. If that's what I have to do to protect Hunter..." my voice trails off for a moment as I let the reality sink in that my moment of happiness is about to expire, "then that's what I will do. After tonight."

"You have no room to..."

"If you know anything about him, you know he isn't going to let me go without a fight. If I leave before he wakes up, it will be easier. Please, Layla, if you care about him half as much as you say you do, then give him tonight. Then I'll be gone."

"You really do care about him, don't you?" Once again, she sounds surprised. I'm not sure if she thinks I'm that heartless or that she's the only one who could possibly love him. Either way, I don't feel the need to voice my feelings for Hunter to her, so I nod. "If this is some sort of attempt to get me to change my mind, it's not going to work."

"I just want tonight. Then, I'm out of his life forever."

"Be gone before he gets up."

I nod again.

This time when I walk to the door, I keep going. I make my way down the hall and straight into Hunter's arms.

"Hey, what's wrong? Are you okay?" he asks as his hand brushes the hair away from my face.

I fight back the tears. I have plenty of time to cry the minute I walk out of his life for good. For now, I just want to enjoy what little time we have left.

"I just missed you," I say as I press a kiss to his lips. "Dance with me?"

"It would be my pleasure." He takes my hand and leads me to the dance floor. We say to the slow ballad that's playing. I'm unfamiliar with the song, but the melody alone has those tears threatening again. "Are you sure everything's okay?"

I hold him a little tighter. "Everything is perfect."

At least for now.

Chapter 32

Hunter

Reaching for my phone on the nightstand, I grab it and check the time. Two hours until we have to leave. That's plenty of time.

I smile as I roll over, ready to reenact every single solitary moment from last night. Quinn was utter perfection. The way she moved the way she moaned. Everything about last night felt like a mixture of the first time and the last time.

My hands reach for her, the bed empty.

Throwing back the covers, I get out of bed and make my way to the bathroom door. I knock softly. "Can I come in?"

No response.

I knock a little louder. "Quinn?"

Still, nothing.

I push open the door without permission. The bathroom is empty. I glance back looking onto the balcony. She isn't there either.

In fact, there isn't a trace of her left in the room.

There's a sinking feeling in my gut that something's off. Something is wrong. With my phone in my hand, I call her. No answer. I call again. Nothing. The texts I send don't get a reply. I slide on a pair of sweats and a shirt and hurry down to Mason's room. I bang on the door until the hungover asshole wakes up.

The door opens and Mason stands before me looking sleep drugged. "What the hell is going on?"

"I can't find Quinn. She won't answer my calls. Something's wrong."

I storm past Mason and into his room not caring what woman he might have in his bed. This is more important. Quinn is more important.

"I'm sure she's fine," Mason says as he shuts the door behind me. "She probably has her phone silenced. I'm sure she just went to get breakfast or something."

Sure, it's a possibility, a good possibility even, but I don't think that's it. Something isn't right, I can feel it.

"No. That's not it. I have a bad feeling Mason." A really bad feeling. Like she's gone. She left me.

"Just take a breath. Relax," he tells me. If the tables were turned, if this was Avery, he wouldn't be so calm.

He dials Quinn's number. No answer.

Though I'm not surprised. If she is unwilling to face me, there is no way she'll face Mason.

"Let's just get home. I'm sure when we get there she'll be sitting on the couch, frustrated that she did what she did."

The feeling of his hand on my shoulder, his attempt to comfort me, doesn't help.

"I'm heading to the airport to see if I can get an earlier flight."

I slam my stuff angrily into my suitcase as I try to figure out what the fuck happened. How we went from making love and professing our feelings to her running on me. Was it too much, too soon? Did she panic? Or was it something else?

The more I think about it, the more it dawns on me how she had seemed off to me last night, during the reception. She went to the bathroom and when she came back, I swear there were tears in her eyes though she denied it.

Still, she hugged me a little tighter. Kissed me a little deeper.

What the hell happened?

"What time's your flight?"

My head snaps in the direction of the voice. A very familiar voice. There's a smile on her face as she steps into the room.

"What did you do?" I shout at Layla.

"What do you mean?" She feigns innocence in asking the question, but I know better. She wouldn't be here right now if she thought Quinn were still here. And if she knows Quinn isn't here, there's a damn good chance that she's the reason behind it all.

"What did you do to Quinn? Did you say something to her? Threaten her?" I stalk toward Layla with a menacing look on my face.

"I... I don't... Hunter," she exclaims as I slam my hand on the wall next to her head.

"What did you do?"

Tears stream down her face, fear in her eyes. "I didn't do it. She did. Ask her."

That's exactly what I intend to do.

The minute the plane lands back in Remington I head straight home. But not to my apartment, to Mason's.

***

"Quinn," I shout as I walk into the apartment that I thankfully have a set of keys to. "Quinn."

I storm toward her room, my hand shoving the door open.

Aside from the bed, it's empty.

She's gone.

She's really gone.

"Is she here?" Mason asks as he steps into the room Quinn has occupied for the last few weeks.

"She's gone."

Chapter 33

Quinn

It's been two weeks since I left the Bahamas. Two long, excruciating weeks since I walked away from the best thing that ever happened to me – Hunter Adams.

Since then, I've been moping and sobbing on Claire's couch because staying with Mason put me in a proximity that was way too close to Hunter. Not to mention, Mason isn't exactly thrilled with me right now. That might actually be an underestimation. He's livid. With right. Not only have I been lying to him, but I've also hurt his best friend.

And I've done all of this without so much as an explanation.

What a mess.

It's better this way, I keep telling myself. It's better because Hunter, he deserves better. He deserves someone whose past won't destroy his future. Still, his words keep running through my head. The ones telling me that nothing will ever change how he feels about me.

Here and now.

It's all he cares about.

It's all I care about too. But when the past can rear its ugly head and potentially destroy the here and now, it's better to just walk away.

The thing I still haven't been able to figure out though, is what the deal with Layla is. Why she would cheat on him, then threaten me to get me away from him? Had she not cheated on him, then I would have never been an issue. They would have been living out their happily ever after. So why go through all of this? For what?

Claire walks through the door to her apartment breaking me of my thoughts.

"Hey," I say in greeting.

"Here," she replies as she drops an envelope on my lap. "I see you still haven't moved off the couch."

"I'll get out of your hair soon," I promise her.

Claire turns and looks at me. "You know I love having you here, Q. But I hate seeing you like this. You need to talk to Hunter. You need to figure out whatever the hell happened between you two."

"There's nothing to figure out," I tell her.

I slide my finger under the seal and open the envelope. I recognize the handwriting immediately – Mason.

Quinn,

I know we're not on the best of terms right now, but when I saw this, I couldn't resist. Take the ticket, go to the show, and seize your opportunity. You deserve more than you realize.

Love,

Mason

"Who's it from?" Claire asks.

"Mason," I reply.

I grab the ticket that had been folded up in the envelope. My mouth drops open.

"What is it?"

"It's a ticket to Mike Flannigan's show – tonight." I contain the shriek of excitement that bubbles up in me. "I can't believe this. I can't believe he would do this."

"Are you going to go?"

I look at the ticket, the opportunity Mason is giving me despite all the screw ups that I've made.

Maybe it's time that I quit feeling sorry for myself, that I quit letting the past affect my future. Hunter is safe now. I can finally face my demons, make my atonements, and move on. Make something out of myself and be what Mason always thought I was – better than our mother, better than the hand we were dealt.

"Hell yeah, I am," I say as I get up from the couch for the first time in what feels like forever and head to the bedroom to figure out what the hell I'm going to wear.

Chapter 34

Hunter

M y eyes dart around the crowded room. I know she's here; I just have to find her.

There is no way in hell she would have been able to resist the ticket to the show, even had it just unexpectedly appeared on her doorstep without so much as an explanation. Just to seal the deal though, I enclosed a letter. It was from me, but I had Mason write it knowing that she wouldn't take anything from me.

Mike Flannigan is her photographic hero.

She's here. I just need to find her.

I grab a drink off the tray of the server passing by me. From what I can see, the guy is talented. Personally, I think Quinn's work is better. I might be a little biased though.

A couple people stop me to chat. People I know, one I didn't, none of them the person that I actually want to talk to.

Weeks of avoidance, weeks of not telling me the truth are about to come to an end. They have to because I'm not sure how much more I can take of this. Quinn Ford disappeared from my life just as quickly as she stormed into it. Thing is, I'm not done with her yet. I don't think I ever will be. Something tells me that she isn't either.

Out of the corner of my eye, I catch her. She's standing before a photograph of an ocean. A woman standing in the sand, her hair blowing in the wind. While I am not much of an art expert, I can clearly see the pain radiating from the woman. Though that might have something to do with the woman who is gazing at it. The woman whose pain I know in great detail. The one I want to hold and help heal and be there for because while she may refuse to acknowledge it, she's amazing.

I move slowly through the room and step behind her. There's enough distance that I'm not touching her, but I'm still close enough to feel her. Christ, how I've missed her.

"I think this one is my favorite," I say.

Her body stills. Motionless she stands there, staring ahead refusing to acknowledge my presence.

"The person looking at it is even better, though."

She turns, slowly, her eyes meeting mine for only a second before darting away. Much like she tries to do with her polite, "Excuse me." The one I refute by stepping in her path and refusing to let her by.

"I've let you go once, Quinn. I won't do it again," I tell her.

"You don't have a choice," she says trying to push past me again. When I don't budge, she becomes angry. "If you don't move, I'm going to cause a scene."

"Cause one, then, because I'm not moving," I reply. I'm calling her bluff and I sure as hell hope I'm right about this. Not that I care much about the attention or people looking, they're going to anyway. "We have unfinished business."

"Me walking out the door, *that* was me finishing it."

I nod, accepting her bullshit reply. "The least you owe me is an explanation."

"I don't owe you anything. I was there doing you a favor. I did it. I left."

Another futile attempt to move past me. "We can keep playing this game, or you can just tell me the truth. Why did you leave, Quinn?"

"Because I was done with you. Satisfied?"

I laugh. "I would be if it were the truth. Try again."

"Not here," she says. This time when she moves, I allow her. What I don't allow is for her to get very far. My fingers reach for her, brushing against her back, to let her know that I'm following, and I don't intend on going anywhere.

She stops abruptly and turns to me. We're alone now in a secluded room. "You did this didn't you? You set me up."

"Did I give you the ticket? Yes. It was meant to be yours. I had planned on the two of us attending together. Regardless of the fact that you left me without so much as a goodbye, I still felt you should be here."

"Well, I am. You can feel free to go now."

An exasperated sigh escapes me. Every fiber of me wants to yell at her, to somehow get through her thick skull that I'm here and I'm not going anywhere. And I don't just mean the show, but in her life.

How do you convince someone of that when everyone in their life that was supposed to love them – abandoned them?

"I'm not going anywhere, Quinn. Not now. Not ever. I'm in this for the long haul. You just have to let me."

"I can't."

"Why not? Tell me what I have to do, and I'll do it."

"I'm doing this for you, Hunter."

How in the hell is keeping us apart doing anything for me except hurting me? As much as I would like to call bullshit, I can tell by the look in her eyes that it isn't.

"There you two are." My mother's voice breaks through the silence filling the air. "Come now, Quinn, we want to introduce you to the man himself."

Quinn's eyes plead with me to get her out of this situation, to help her. I am helping her though, the best way I know how. Whether or not she wants to be with me, this is her chance. An opportunity for her to pursue the one thing that I am certain she loves. Instead of speaking up and asking my mother to leave us alone, I step to the side. I allow my mother to take her hand and lead her away as I follow.

"Mike, darling," my mother says. "I want you to meet someone."

The man standing with my father laughing, suddenly stops when his eyes fall on Quinn. "And who do we have here?"

"This is the young woman I was telling you about, Quinn Ford. She's exceptionally talented and I think would be a wonderful intern for you," my mother gushes.

Quinn's cheeks flush at the compliment. "It's an honor to meet you, Mr. Flannigan. I absolutely love your work."

He nods his head toward one of his photos. "What about this one? What do you think of it?"

Quinn's head turns to the side as she studies it. "It's striking. You've really managed to catch the essence of..."

While she studies the photo, I study her. Her poise, her knowledge, her body. Each one another reason to add to the pile of reasons for why I admire and love her. Because I do love her. And not being with her, not seeing where this could go, it's killing me.

"You have quite an eye," Mike's deep voice says breaking my thoughts. "I would love to pick your brain more and see your work. Could we meet on Monday at my studio?"

"Yes, I'd love that," Quinn says. Her voice is filled with a tempered excitement, not the squeal that I am certain she would prefer to let out.

"I'll see you then," he says. "If you'll excuse me, I have buyers to schmooze."

Quinn turns to my parents, her eyes welling with tears. "Thank you, Mr. and Mrs. Adams. You've made my dream come true."

"And you've made ours as well," my mother says as she pats her hand against Quinn's arm. "We'll see you two later."

When they're gone, Quinn turns to me. "You didn't tell them?" I shake my head. "Why not?"

"I was holding out hope," I admit.

"Hunter."

"I'll make you a deal." She folds her arms in front of her as she stares at me. "If you tell me why, the real reason why, I will leave you alone for good. If that's what you want." My hand touches her cheek. "Please, Quinn. It's killing me. Do you have any idea how pathetic I looked standing in the corner over there pining away for you?"

A smile cracks through her stoic façade. "I thought you didn't pine?"

"Not over a woman like Layla. But you? I'm pining. Hard."

"You're not going to like what I have to say," she tells me. The funny thing is, I don't care what her reason is. The only reason I need to know is, so I know how to fix it, or dispel it, or whatever it is that I need to do. Whatever it takes to get her back.

"There really isn't much about you that I don't like."

"We'll see about that," she says.

Chapter 35

Quinn

When I walked out of the gallery, my intention was to head to a bar, to a restaurant, anywhere but where we ended up. A hotel. Not just any hotel, but *the* hotel. The place that started all of this. The bar, which just like that night, is mostly quiet.

There is one significant difference this time though.

We don't hate each other. In fact, I think we both love each other. I down the drink in front of me needing the courage it will bring. When I set the glass on the table, his hand reaches for mine.

"What is it, baby? What happened?" The deep, but soft timber of his voice lulls me into a sense of security. One that will most likely be pulled out from under me the minute I tell him the truth.

"It's Shane." There is hurt in his eyes. "No, it's not what you think. I didn't leave you for him. Hell, I am pretty sure I stopped caring about him the minute you found me in this bar." I glance down at where his fingers meet my skin. That wasn't the best start to this conversation. I wasn't prepared though. Walking into that gallery tonight, the last thing I expected was Hunter, let alone being back here with him.

"Then what is it?" The gentle sound carries undertones of a frustration that he is more than entitled too.

"You were right, he's the reason I had to leave Columbia. Him and the scandal I was involved in." I can practically see the gears in his head turning. What kind of scandal? What could she have done? Yet, I don't think what I am about to tell him is anywhere in the realm of what he's expecting. "He was my professor, and we were... we were dating, Hunter."

The slightest of weights lifts from my chest. The secret that had been gnawing at me is about to be exposed. While I should want to keep it hidden, want to make sure that he doesn't hate me, the relief I feel from that small admission feels so good that it urges me to continue.

"He was my, very married, professor."

Hunter shakes his head in what I can only imagine is disbelief. "No. You wouldn't do that."

"I did. I was with him and..."

"You knew he was married and you still..."

"I had no idea he was married. Not until she showed up in class and slapped me across the face."

Hunter's head turns to the side, his eyes imploring me, trying to figure out the story that I've only given him in pieces so far.

"Let me start over. Shane was my professor. He was helping me with a project and we uh... well, you get the idea. The relationship continued after the project was over. His wife somehow found out about us and stormed into class and slapped me. I deserved every bit of her anger. Intentional or not, I was the other woman, I wrecked her marriage."

"But you didn't know," Hunter says as if that tiny little snippet of information somehow makes it all okay.

"Anyway, rumors started flying, everyone was talking. The school started looking into my grades, assuming that I had slept my way to my 4.0 GPA. While they couldn't prove anything, the suspicion was still there. That's when the school decided it would be best if I left."

"And this professor of yours?"

"He's still there. As far as I know at least."

"Jesus, Quinn," Hunter says as he runs his hand through his hair. "I'm sorry. That's... awful."

"Thank you. But as you can see, I'm fine. In large part, thanks to you."

"Why didn't you just tell me? I told you, baby, nothing about your past is going to change how I feel about you."

"I was scared. Afraid you would think that I was just like Layla, and that when you realized it, you would hate me. But that's not why I left. I left for you Hunter. Not because of you."

"You're talking in circles. Just... tell me already."

I look into his eyes one last time. Because as soon as I tell him this, if he doesn't send me away on his own, then I need to walk away. I refuse to hurt him anymore than I have and me and my reputation, my mistakes, my screwed-up life could only do that – hurt him.

"I left because if that information were to be leaked, if someone found out about my past, my childhood, the incident with Shane, or one of my countless other screw ups it could ruin things up for you. You could lose endorsements. Your charity would suffer. I can't do that. I can't risk that. You've worked so damn hard to build this life for yourself, I refuse to be the one to make it come crumbling down."

"How in the hell would anyone find out? And even if they did... I don't care. I don't care what anyone thinks. We'll figure out a way to make it work."

"Layla knows. She knows everything and..."

Hunter's hand hits the bar with a thud. His face that was calm only moments ago is a bright shade of anger driven red. I stare at him half expecting smoke to billow from his ears.

"I appreciate the concern, Quinn, but you shouldn't be taking advice from Layla. As it turns out her whole relationship with Maddox was bullshit. Nothing more than a means to get him to sign with her at the sports new agency she joined. Seems once he was officially signed, she was going to try to get back together with me. But you got in the way."

"I know what she did was unethical, but..."

"Her reputation would be ruined. She would never work as a sports agent again," he says. "Trust me. We do not have anything to worry about from her."

"It's not worth the risk."

"Like hell it isn't," he argues.

The anger subsides, his focus returning to me. The tips of his fingers gently swiping away the tears that began to fall.

"Did you not hear me when I told you that I love you? Do you not understand what those words mean? What they mean to me?" He pulls me to him and takes my face in his hands. He forces me to look into his eyes and see what it is he's feeling since I won't believe his words. "I love you, Quinn. Every piece of you. Every secret. Every fault. I love that you make me laugh. I love that you drive me crazy. I love that you fight with me because even when we're fighting it means you're still there. That's what I care about. If my endorsers want to drop me, fine. If the charity goes under, I'll figure something out. If I get kicked off the damn team – I don't care. Because none of it, not a single damn thing, matters if I'm not going to have you next to me."

"How can you say that?" I sob. "We were together a week, Hunter. How can you be so sure that I'm worth throwing everything away for?"

"It's been more than a week, Quinn. It's been fifteen years. We just needed that extra little push to see it. Don't you get it? That's what that week was – our push."

I rise from my seat, stepping between his legs. "I'm afraid if we do this, if you lose everything, you'll resent me."

"I could never resent you. And at the risk of sounding like I'm negating your feelings here; you're making a bigger deal out of this then necessary. Layla played you. She played on your fears. Fear that I would hate you, fear that you're not good enough. None of which is true."

His hands grip my hips tugging me flush against him.

"I... I love you Hunter. I never want...."

His lips press against mine, the tender kiss escalating quickly. Weeks apart driving our need for each other. When he pulls back, I realize he's right. Because in that one kiss I felt more alive than I have in weeks. I'm filled with hope and happiness. How in the hell did I let that woman get in my head? How did I let her nearly destroy the only thing that has ever truly made me happy?

"I don't deserve you," I tell him. "But I sure as hell am willing to prove myself every damn day. I love you, Hunter. I don't want to be without you anymore."

Epilogue

Quinn

The sky is blue, sun is shining, and Hunter is on the field. I swear, I never thought life could be like this. Happy, fulfilling – good. But it is. And it's all because of number 92.

The game is nearing its end. The Red Devils are up by seven and if they win this, they're on to the Superbowl. I cheer loudly as the play begins and jump out of my seat.

"Go, Hunter." I scream out the words as Avery cheers for Mason next to me. It's been our ritual throughout the season.

The play ends and my eyes drift to the clock. Thirty seconds left. I cross my fingers, my toes, everything but my legs. My mind drifts momentarily to how Hunter's strong hands spread them this morning. How his head sank between them. Yeah, he definitely wouldn't want me crossing those.

This is it. A tackle. A block. A clock down to zero and the Red Devil's seal their spot in the Superbowl! Avery and I hug each other as we jump up and down with joy. While the rest of the crowd remains in their spots, Avery and I begin to sneak off. We don't have to watch the happenings on the field. We get to enjoy the real celebration.

As we pass by the concession stand, I stop in my tracks at the sound of my name and the even more familiar voice that's saying it. I can't believe my ears. When I turn, my gaze falling on the one man I thought I would never lay eyes on again, I smile. Not because it's him, not because I remotely care anymore, but rather, because I don't.

Shane Powell doesn't mean a thing to me. He wasn't good or kind. He was an asshole.

Hunter was right. If I quit dating assholes, I might realize what the difference was. And then, he showed me.

"Shane." I say his name. My voice is completely void of emotion. In fact, I'm not even sure why I am standing here. I should be headed to Hunter, the only man that matters. I wonder momentarily, what Hunter would say. Would he tell me turn and walk away? Or would he tell me to take control, to show this insignificant piece of shit exactly what he means to me.

"I can't believe it's you. How have you been?" His eyes light up, his smile broader than I have ever seen it.

"I'm amazing," I tell him. "School is going great, I have an internship with Mike Flannigan, and..." I pause to admire the look of shock and jealousy that rises out of what I'm telling him. Take that jackass. "I have an amazing boyfriend who is waiting on me."

"Are you as happy with him as you were with me?" Shane says taking a step closer.

"Happier. A real happiness. Not the fake bullshit that you lured me into."

"Quinn..."

"Don't Quinn me. What you did, Shane, to me and to your wife, was wrong. Wrong on so many damn levels."

"It's not what it looked like. Amber..."

"How is Amber by the way?" I ask.

"I don't know. She left me."

The amount of satisfaction I get from that feels wrong. I shouldn't be pleased that his wife left him, that his world crumbled. But the satisfaction I feel isn't in regard to him, it's for Amber. Good for her for leaving. Good for her for taking charge of her life and not putting up with a cheating asshole of a husband.

"You know, Shane, I really think this whole situation worked out for the best."

I begin to walk away but he grabs my arm.

"I wouldn't do that if I were you," I tell him.

"Why is that?"

"Because her boyfriend really doesn't like when other men have their hands on her." The deep voice coming from behind Shane startles both of us. He should be on the field, not standing here.

Yet, here he is. Sweaty and dirty and sexy as hell.

"You can either let her go," Hunter says. "Or I can make you let her go. The choice is yours."

Shane lets go of my arm, his hand dropping to his side. "I didn't... I wasn't..."

"I don't care what you were or weren't doing. All I care about is that you stay the hell away from her. Understood?"

Shane nods.

"Good. You should probably get going." A crowd begins to form around us. Not because they care about me or Shane or our drama. But because every single one of them adores the man in the shoulder pads and football jersey. Almost as much as I do.

"Like I said. Happier." Those are the last words I say to Shane before walking straight into Hunter's arms. "I am so proud of you, baby."

He scoops me into his arms bringing me eye level with him. "I love you, Quinn."

Seeing Shane again. Being in this moment with Hunter. Nothing in the world has ever seemed so clear.

This is where I am supposed to be.

If this is where every damn thing that I have ever had to endure in my life led me, I would do it again in a heartbeat.

There is no place like Hunter's arms.

About L.M. Reid

L.M. Reid is a reader, writer, and lover of all things romance. Just a girl from the Midwest with simple tastes and dirty thoughts. If she's not busy clicking away at her laptop with an iced coffee in hand, she can be found at home surrounded by hot wheels and the love of her husband and son.

Book Bub: http://scarlet.pub/LMBB
Facebook (Page): https://scarlet.pub/LMFB
Instagram: https://scarlet.pub/LMIG
Goodreads: https://scarlet.pub/LMGR
And don't forget to join my reader group!
L.M. Reid's Steamy Romance Readers: https://scarlet.pub/LMGroup

Also By L.M. Reid

The Making the Play Series

Playing the Game
Playing the Field
Playing to Win
Played Out

The Hard to Love Series

Hard to Hate
Hard to Trust
Hard to Forgive

Check out all my new releases at:
www.scarletlanternpublishing.com/lmreid

Made in the USA
Monee, IL
10 February 2022

90152193R10111